HOVIS BROWN

BY

PETER HARRISON

First published by Barny Books

ISBN No: 978.1.903172.91.9

Publishers: Barny Books
                 Hough on the Hill
                 Grantham
                 Lincolnshire
                 NG32 2BB

                 Tel: 01400 250246
                 www.barnybooks.biz

Dedicated to

Nora

Sweetest girl in the world

Acknowledgments

My great thanks go to

Molly Burkett and Jayne Thompson

for all their help and support

CHAPTER ONE

Present Day

The phone-call was garbled, agitated and definitely female, didn't know if she wanted the police or the ambulance......*Seen him a few times climbing on the wall. Not my wall, next door. Climbed on the wall the night before last and sat there a few minutes. Whose wall? ... the fish-shop of course, my next door neighbour, sat like a big lummox watching the flat and the back of the shop then he up and left, third time this week..."*

"Which service would you require, Madam?"

I'm getting there! The woman was annoyed now. *Done the same about half an hour ago, closing-time at the shop. Opened the door to let Trixie in – that's my cat - saw him again, only this time he jumped in the back-yard. No, their yard, Warren Fisheries, only I heard the door to the flat open and shut, reckon he was up to no good....*

"Which service...."

Heard a shot! I was having a smoke, shop-lights went out, maybe a minute later there was a shot, heard a window breaking! You'd better send someone, think someone has been killed!

"Connecting you Madam."

I told the girl, officer, Horden opposite Geordies Pizza shop, near the Fairworld Bingo? It was a gun-shot; better get down here quick, all hell's broken loose!

Norma Blackwood, cigarette in one hand and the fat grey cat in the other, moved to her back-door again and called out, "Joan, pet, it's Norma, I've called the police-station. Joan, are you okay?"

Minutes later and a patrol car screeched to a halt outside *Geordies.* One officer bolted from the vehicle and ran along the small alley that separated the pizza parlour and the Indian takeaway. His companion hurried into the busy front shop shouting, "Police! Keep calm, the building is surrounded!"

Behind the counter, Louise Fletcher couldn't hide her displeasure, glanced at Chantelle Old, "I told you my birthday is next week, Chantelle," she said above the din "and I told you no Strippergram!"

Two large police cruisers, tyres screaming in protest skidded from the main coastal road and roared past the *Trust* pub, stopped next to one another blocking the smaller back-road. P.C. Jeffries scrambled from his vehicle, saw the damaged window above the shop, the littered fragments of broken glass strewn across the pavement and shouted to the other car, "I'll take the back-door, you take the front!" Then he stopped dead in his tracks.

From the side street a huge figure walked slowly towards the patrol cars. Big as a house-end, the fellow cradled the figure in his arms, his head nudging and kissing the clinging woman, whispered soothing comforting words as the female wept softly.

"Don't move!" shouted the lone officer.

The second car vomited another policeman who held aloft a truncheon, "Stay where you are, put down the woman, now!"

Running frantically from the pizza-shop, across the busy main-road almost careering with a *Red-Stripe* taxi, the original patrolman, P.C. Jason Bright, screamed a warning to his colleagues, "Someone has been shot!"

Jackie Brown said to the woman, "Pantomime policemen have arrived Joan," squeezed her lovingly. "Shall I put you down, pet?"

"Give me a cuddle, you big fool," she fondled his hair, wiped her eyes on his jacket and kissed his whiskered features.

"On the ground, now!" barked another officer.

A distance away, cars braked, howled and shuddered to a halt as a policeman trundled across the road. P. C. Marty Aldridge was sodden, flaccid and smelling of dog-shit. He had slipped in the dark exterior of *Geordies*, ran into a dilapidated fence and fell into a festering pool of discarded petrol and excrement. The crestfallen cop crossed the road, both hands held aloft, ordering the traffic to slow.

"Over here, Marty!" bellowed his buddy, "it's this shop. We got it wrong!"

"Better put me down, Jackie," said the woman, "I'll try and explain."

"Right!" shouted an officer witnessing the compliance, "now let her walk away and there'll be no trouble!"

Another policeman bellowed, "On the deck, now!"

"Go fuck yourself!" said the giant. "The roads are filthy!"

*****

The following afternoon

The conference room was choc-a-block. Standing directly in front of the big screen Detective Inspector Ruth Stanger held the file close to her chest. She took a deep breath and started to address her men.

"Lights!" and the uniformed officer dimmed the switch, plunging the room into darkness. The Inspector moved to one side as her second in command, D.S. Tommy Butler started the slide-show.

The first picture showed the crumpled bloody remains of the large male, face contorted in death, eyes wide as if disbelieving, dentures loose and filled with black/red blood. Shaven-headed and battle-scarred, Michael Bruen, even in death, had the capacity to instill fear and respect. There were sighs and whispers from the selected audience, all hardened career men and women who had seen all the

7

muck and horror of life. They were the first to see the mortal remains of the London gangster. They murmured in disgust.

"Picture One: Approximately 24 hours old, Michael Edward Bruen, born 1947, Chiswick, West London. Height: 6 feet 2 inches; 240 pounds. Moved to Acton, W3: approximately 1961. Petty theft, progressing to robbery with violence. Usual apprenticeship, moved up the ladder when he started using his fists for a living. Worked Hammersmith for Leroy Jackson, pulled more than once for breaking bones. No convictions until he moves to Ealing and works the doors for James McGovern, loses his temper one night and puts some unlucky punter in a coma. Five years lock-up in Durham and one week into the sentence he's almost killed. On a life-support for a week, steel-plate in his skull, extensive internal injuries to the whole of the body, Severe distortion of the groin area, no witnesses. One name."

D.I. Stanger put down her notes. The lights came on.

"The attack was frenzied and prolonged. Michael Edward Bruen almost died. The injury to the groin area?" She cleared her throat, wanted the next part over with fast, "The man's penis was severed," already she was flushing, "sorry, part-severed." She composed herself, stared around the male-dominated room, "As this attack happened in the lavatory-area, the over-riding view was that it was homosexual in its origins, maybe a rejection. Bruen at the time was unmarried."

Josh White, veteran of twenty years in the force, was a clever man but uncouth and impatient. "Should castrate all the bent bastards, Gov, got some leads?" Turning to Millicent Howden he said loud enough for all to hear. "Boy George is a queer, Martina Navratilova is a queer. What is the world coming to Milly?"

"Keep that for the canteen Josh!" growled the chief. She waited, deliberately milking the silence. "Right, Albert

8

Quinlan, the butcher from Brighton. Cut up his wife in 1972 - serving life?" Half a dozen heads nodded acknowledgement. "Notorious homosexual was pulled and released, everything points to him for the attack."

A nod to the uniform and the lights dimmed again. The image showed the gruesome blood-soaked chest area of the dead man. "Exit wound. The shell was a 2.2 long-stem; kill anyone up to half a mile. Close range though. Forensics claims the impact and angle make it a certainty that the killer was across the street from the flat. Straight through the heart."

"Professional hit?" came a voice from the audience.

"Pointing to a professional hit," agreed the D.I. "Picture three. Entry wound!" The minute tear through the jacket was barely noticeable, a faint touch of crimson tainted the material. Another hand signal from the officer and the lights came on.

"Motive, Gov?" Detective Gordon Carr, newly promoted, was shaking his head in disbelief. "There's something not right."

Ruth Stanger shrugged her slim shoulders. "Not the usual Friday night punch-up outside the *Trust*?"

"Horden…The Bronx!" laughed Moses Butler, a new kid on the block, B.Sc.(Hons). Everybody knew if Moses could have printed his qualifications on toilet-paper he would have done. He stopped smiling, "Gordon's hit the nail on the head. The shop, the new owners and how did he get into the flat?"

"Why was he in the flat?" asked Gordon Carr.

Dennis Armitage, a year from retirement, a D.C. for twenty years was quiet, intense, clever too, he spoke softly to his superior. "One of my snitches tells me that Michael Bruen has been living in the *Trust* for a few days, bed and board, same man tells me that Bruen called on Ryan Dimonti a few days ago. I don't know why."

"Dimonti?" said D.I. Stanger, crunching her face, "another refugee from the Bronx?" She eyed Moses Butler. "Opinions?"

"Bad boy, drugs, collections, always has a bunch of heavies to do his dirty work but murder? Not Ryan Dimonti."

"Names of these heavies?"

"Percy Willetts is one but he's downstairs in the cells, put his wife in traction again".

"And the other?"

"Jackie Brown, crackerjack from Hartlepool, a right animal, maimed a few in his time."

Dennis Armitage spoke again. "Something else boss, little bird tells me Jackie Brown had a fall-out with Dimonti. Jackie Brown leaves: Micky Bruen arrives?"

Ruth Stanger smiled, saved the best news till last. "Owner of the shop and flat is a Miss Joan Belling. Guess who her fiancé happens to be?"

"Give me a clue, boss," said Moses Butler with a faint smile on his face. "Is he tall, dark and handsome?"

"Definitely tall," answered the D.I. "but as for handsome…"

CHAPTER TWO

One year earlier.

Jackie 'Hovis' Brown hadn't long finished his day stint with Hudson's Taxis, the biggest private-hire firm in Hartlepool. He'd worked there months. It wasn't a bad job as jobs go, better than the factory work before that, more money and a lot more freedom. What really upset him was the lack of skirt available. It should have been pussy-on-a-plate but he hadn't even a whiff! Didn't bother him too much, pleased enough to be back on his home turf. Never did get used to bloody Horden Colliery, too many crazy colliers for his liking. Queer buggers too, cursed the job until they were blue in the face and spent all their time talking about the damn coal-mine. Their women were total morons, could drive a man crazy: drove Hovis crazy. He'd had his day with them. Especially one. Women! Manipulating and controlling, used men to suit their own means, all whores, every last one. *Mess with Hovis Brown and you're dead meat*, he thought. He smiled to himself. *Mess with me and see what happens*! Felt good.

He eased his six foot eight frame on to the bonnet of his rust-bucket of a motor and the Vauxhall groaned with the weight. He was contemplating visiting his mother and then he pictured his parent and her newest beau, felt so sick he wanted to throw up. His mother was fifty years old, looked sixty and acted like a teenager. Doris Brown! When he was a kid, he'd heard her other name: Dirty Doris Brown. They'd lived in and around Hartlepool for most of their lives, Doris Brown and her son, Jackie. He was always told he'd been named after his father but that was another lie because he never met his dad and there were no photographs of him. His earliest memories were of his Ma and him, on their own. Every time he had tried to talk about his father he was ignored or verbally abused. *Shut up, Jackie! Leave it alone!* His Mother couldn't get through a day without lying. *Named after my Father, that'll be the day!*

It was his Ma's fault for being labelled and lumbered with such a stupid name, he blamed her; she blamed the *Hovis* bread advertisements on the television at the time. *Brains for bread*, his mother would scold whenever he was out of favour. The name stuck, very few people called him by his correct name, only Anna. Anna always called him Jackie or Big Jack. Made him feel proud.

He pulled out cigarettes and lighter, sucked in the smoke like he was deflating a *Zeppelin* and eased off the decrepit motor, walked a pace and leaned against the steel safety barrier. Jackie gazed at the thrashing ocean, saw and heard the frenzied calls of the sea-gulls as they ducked and dived and fought above the foaming waves. To his left he saw the forlorn and neglected pier, the lone angler pitching his line, oblivious to the swell and pulsating lift as the sea battered the esplanade. Before him, Hartlepool Bay, the second largest bay in the country, naked and raw as the wind rocked and battered the shoreline. No boats or yachts or pleasure craft today as nature screamed its presence. Jackie Brown looked ahead as the cool spray splattered his body, across the wide expanse of ocean towards Redcar and, in the distance, the dipping undulating cliffs of Whitby and Scarborough, so close and yet so far away. *As the crow flies*, smiled the man. Never visited as a child, no one to take him, but when he was older, when he was a grown man, he had taken Anna, took her everywhere and anywhere she asked. They were the happiest days of his life.

He pictured his Ma and thought about the early days. It was every month that his mother would be introducing another *uncle* to him. Sometimes two at a time and it was always after she'd been out at the pub. *Go outside and play,*

Hovis. I'm entertaining your Uncle Tom or Dick or Harry.
Then he would get a little upset. *Got no friends, Ma, can't I stay in with you?* It was like talking to a brick wall as he was unceremoniously thrown out of his own house by either his agitated mother or one of his *uncles.* His mother's favourite haunt was next to the train-station. The *Devon* was a notorious dive then. It still was a pick-up palace.

The first time he'd seen his Mother intimate with another man was an earth-shattering experience. He had mooched about the entry-door of the pub, even resorted to asking the punters to tell his mother to come out. She was nowhere to be seen so Hovis had wandered, ended up at the rear of the pub, not intentionally looking for his parent. Hovis thought he was Jack-the-lad, steal anything that wasn't bolted down, that's when he'd heard the commotion: the grunting and the *bump-bump* of the couple trying not to unhinge the metal dustbin that was being used as a temporary bed. Walked right in amongst the piles of crates and pallets and saw the woman leaning, doggy-fashion, across the steel container, skirts pushed all the way up to her skinny rumpled arse. One of her stockings clinging helplessly on to the suspender-belt for dear life, the other, crumpled and at half-mast. He stood as stiff as a statue, eyes wide and mouth open, he'd seen dogs on heat doing such disgusting things but never real people.
Then the shock as the female turned her sweating gasping face towards her son. Doris, doped on a heady mix of *Budweiser* and *Valium,* started laughing. Then the man twisted his huge ponderous belly and leered, asked him if he wanted a ride on his Mammy! Little Jackie was dumb with shock, unable to speak, watching as the beefy individual struggled impatiently trying to find some change from his pockets. He still remembered his mother's words, not what he had expected. *Hovis, son, run to the fish-shop and buy three lots,* adding seriously *and Hovis, take your*

time. His own mother, laughing hysterically as he bolted. There were scores of repeated incidents, with scores of different *uncles.* It sickened him, sickened him to his soul. Sometimes, even now, he had nightmares about his Ma.

Not a lot of luck ever came his way, especially with relationships. Time and time again he had been used and then discarded, his brusque manner, his guttural humour, even his size tended to put women off. *You're a dumb oaf, Jackie,* Anna had said but he always imagined he was going to be her dumb oaf for the rest of his life. He was so sure, their rapport was ideal. Hovis fell deeply in love, courted her for long enough, became a willing slave for the petite, blue-eyed, blonde, Anna Belling.

Hovis could never forget her words, *Will you look after me, Jackie? Will you always protect me*? And, of course, he promised, meant it like he'd never meant it before. Whatever she wanted, she got, spent all of his money on her. Lavished gifts on her, nothing he wouldn't do for Anna, even when she demanded the two young scalps. *They were awful to me, Jackie,* she'd whined. *Tried to assault me, Jackie. You've gotta do it for me Jackie.* Pups they were and of course he followed her instructions. *Bang bang*! Who could beat Jackie Brown? Trouble was he used a little too much force, blinded one and crippled the other, felt bad about it at the time, felt worse when he was locked up in Durham jail for two damn years. He should have left it alone after the bust-up at the dance-hall. He'd kicked hell out of the two kids, done enough he'd thought but no, Anna Belling wanted more blood, made him wait outside the building until they showed their bloodied faces. Talked about it like it was the *Battle of Little Big Horn,* he was Custer and the youths were the Indians only he was definitely going to win. He would take their scalps because Anna was livid, persuading him to finish the job. *Get them, Jackie! Get them for me, Jackie!*

Then the bloody shame, only days out of jail and the realisation that Anna was seeing another man, shocked him to his core. He dealt with the problem the only way he knew how, started a fight with the diminutive, skinny punk. *You know who I am, sonny?* He screamed at the stranger. *Walk away while you can walk!* His threats usually worked, scared the opposition into defeat. Who could beat Jackie Brown? He had never lost a fight in his life. Until that day, then Hovis's world went *upside-down*. The total and utter humiliation when that under-sized collier destroyed his world. Until that day, he thought he was unbeatable, his size scared the hell out of most people. He could still not believe it, not from the little bastard! And the worst thing was Anna Belling looking at him with such contempt, disgust written all over her face, like he was something she'd found on the bottom of her shoe! Left him there, battered and bruised on the ground and walked away with the smiling peacock.

He'd begged her to rekindle the relationship, pleaded as if his very life depended on it and in some ways it did. The man did not believe he could live without the Horden girl. It frightened him, alone in the lock-up, trying to visualize life without Anna. He'd spent a year in Durham nick, appealed and won, still a bloody nightmare. Wasn't the fact that the *porridge* was hard-going, it was the loss of his love, the unbelievable despair at her absence. Twelve horrendous months with only his mother showing her painted face when she felt like it. Not once did Anna show her beautiful face. He wrote to her once a week without fail. Albert Quinlan, who shared a cell with him, helped him compose the letters. Albert, a lifer, had butchered his missus when he found out she was having an affair with Henry Johnstone, caught the pair of them in his bed when he returned home early from a night out with the boys. *So why didn't you kill him as well?* asked a confused Hovis Brown. *He was my best friend,* said an irate Albert Quinlan.

Now do you want me to compose the bloody letter or not? So the letters were sent. Every Saturday morning they would sit in the prison library and write the love letters. She never replied, not once. Didn't stop Hovis. Later, when he re-read the composition alone in his cell, he would smile at the words; it was as if he were talking to Anna, kept him alive for another day. Never missed one single week in the whole year he was behind bars, the image of Anna kept his flagging spirit alive.

When his sentence was over he left the lock-up more in love with her than before. Then he heard the news, standing like a big pudding knocking at the locked door in Handley Street in Horden and the neighbour sticking her head out of her door. *She's seeing someone else, Hovis, love.* Even knew his name and where he lived. *Marlon McGintey! West Avenue. On the hill, above the graveyard in Easington.* Knew everybody's bloody business, did Ivy Roundtree. *Marlon! Marlon! What kind of name was that? Actor was he? On the Waterfront, eh, I'll drown the little bastard!* But Marlon McGintey was a pit-bull. And Jackie, Jackie Brown was a great soft St. Bernard, lost the only fight in his life to someone half his size and weight. Incomprehensible to Jackie Brown, thought he'd lost the fight and his only love, told himself that Anna was a thing of the past.

With hindsight, Jackie should have run a mile from the scheming female but he could not resist, not for a moment, couldn't visualise life without Anna. Weeks later and the phone call came from the colliery; Anna had sickened of her new love and had unceremoniously ditched him. Jackie thought that he was again in favour, handed in his resignation at the *Sca* cardboard factory in Hartlepool and drove all the way to the terraced house in Handley Street. *Their home again*, he thought, taking it easy, not showing too much enthusiasm being around Anna. The last thing in the world he wanted to do was to upset the girl, too precious a commodity to him, made his world go round, hurt his head so bad week after week, month after month, but Jackie Brown persevered and eased his way gently back into her life.

It was not like before, even he knew that as Anna shamelessly used and abused him. *Do this for me, Jackie. Do that for me, Jackie,* until he was demented. Daily torture, that's what it was. *I'm going out with the girls tonight, Jackie,* she would inform him as if it were a perfectly natural thing to do. *Don't ask, Jackie! I'll be back when I feel like it,* making him feel so small. Six feet eight and feeling small! Nice to him some days, like it was the old times back with a vengeance and then suddenly, ignoring his presence and mute for hours, in the same house but as if he didn't exist, making him ill the way she mistreated him. He became that piece of muck stuck on her boots, right down to the smell! Time and time again she would torment him with her bizarre and odd eccentricities. *See you, Jackie,* then she'd start singing some old tune, *Don't know where, don't know when.* A regular Vera Lynn she was, laughing at him without fear of reprisal. *Get back to Third Street now, there's a package to pick up. Pay them will you, Jackie, love, I'll square with you later.* She never did of course and his meagre benefit money didn't last a bloody day.

He had to find work, any work, just as long as it was fiddle; cash in hand. That's when he met Ryan Dimonti, drug-dealer, thief and landlord. Local boy made good, always needed heavies to enforce his nefarious business scams. Who was bigger or heavier than Hovis Brown? He called at Dimonti's house and was immediately deployed on collection duties. Easy money for Jackie, the cash went straight into Anna's purse, *You're no good with money, Jackie. I'll take care of it,* said Anna Belling.

Then one day, out of the blue, she told him she wanted to live on her own, on a whim. *Jackie, you gotta understand, things change, love. I'm nearly eighteen and I feel, well, sorta closed in. It's like we're husband and wife, Jackie.* She could be as steel once her mind was made up and no matter how he tried he couldn't dissuade her. *Who'll pay the rent, Anna, who'll buy the food?* It was like talking to a stranger. *Stop with the puppy-dog eyes, Jackie. You know I don't like scenes, okay?* Then she offered him a life-line, of sorts. *Jackie. You want, I'll phone you now and then. It's only Hartlepool, you're talkin' ten minutes ride away. I'll phone you....or maybe you can phone me, eh and then you can call for me and we'll have some time together. What you say, Jackie, least this way, we'll still see each other?*

What could he say; he was butter in her hands, better now and then than never. Jackie wasn't such a fool, sometimes he could act the part of a clown but he wasn't stupid. He knew that she had met with someone again, knew he was in the way, so he left without a word of protest. He could never intentionally hurt Anna. He imagined the rest of his life being her play-thing; a pawn for Anna Belling, discarded like a Christmas puppy when February comes along, maybe taken for the occasional walk when the summer was long and inviting. He left without a fight, not even a whimper, wanted to ask who her new beau was, wondered if it were the infamous Marlon McGintey coming back into her life again. Jackie was too proud to ask.

Jackie Brown did return to Horden, sometimes once a week, sometimes monthly. It wasn't Anna who called, it was like he was back in prison again, no phone-calls, no letters, zilch. Dimonti called him. Sometimes visited Horden or Peterlee, anywhere really, went where he was told. Ryan Dimonti gave the instructions and the enforcer completed the task with vengeance and zeal. He would punish people thinking he was punishing Anna, kept him

18

sane, kept him alive. *I'm sorry, Mr. Dimonti, it got a little outa hand is all, but he'll not be late with his rent again. Any time, Mr. Dimonti, you can call me night and day. Hudson's Taxi's? Not a problem, I make more one night for you than a week on the taxis. Call me anytime, Mr. Dimonti.*

He liked working away from Hartlepool, loved it when he had to call on some skip-rat in Horden for Ryan Dimonti. Gave him a chance to mooch around certain streets, there was always the slim chance he would meet Anna Belling. Slim was the wrong word, had a better chance winning the football-pools. Months had gone by and not a sight nor sound of her. She was still around, knew that for a fact, had occasionally driven past her house. The lights were usually on and sometimes the curtains were half-closed and Jackie could see the television-screen. *Television switched on and working*! He surmised Anna was still about, wanted to see her, a glimpse would ease his mind.

CHAPTER THREE

Bill and Mildred Belling had lived in Horden all of their married life. Bill, born and bred in nearby Easington Colliery, had met his future wife-to-be when she, together with her best friend, Dinah Handy, had visited the weekly dance at the Easington Welfare Hall. Lots of youngsters, from the gawky thirteen year-olds to the street-wise seventeen year-olds filled the place to capacity. Bill, eighteen and two years older than the pouting and very available Mildred, decided that the young virgin, *You're the first, Bill,* was going to be his bride. Six months to the day and the couple wed and moved to Horden Colliery. Bill transferred mines and settled down immediately. Milly, three months pregnant, recommenced her wayward ways as soon as the nuptials were over. Bill worked a three-shift system at the pit: first-shift, back-shift and night-shift. Milly regularly worked the night-shift. *Fish and chips again, Milly*? was his regular grouse. *Geordie's Pizza*? Night-shift for Bill was synonymous with fast-food. He was probably the only one in the local vicinity who didn't know about Milly's extra-marital activities.

Within three years, 1960 to 1963, three beautiful daughters were born but only the first child could truly carry the name of Belling. The paternity of the other two came from the vast untapped genetic pool of Horden's finest. Bill's only gripe was the gender of the offspring. Still he counted his blessings, three girls and all healthy. Joan, Milly junior and last but not least, Anna. The youngest became the most vociferous and the most outspoken of the three. The system stayed fairly stable until the youngest, Anna, reached her teens. Granite-hard with a tongue to match any collier, she soon exerted her rightful place at the front of the queue.

Anna was only four years old when she was abused for the very first time. Uncle Tyler, Milly Belling's youngest brother was baby-sitting at the time. Daddy at work, mummy out on the prowl and Tyler Chandler simultaneously watching a seedy video whilst gazing wide-eyed at the inside cover of *Penthouse* and trying to masturbate left-handed when little Anna stumbled into the sitting-room. *Bad dream, Uncle Tyler*, she'd said, then she observed the small erection emanating from the groin area of her favourite uncle. *What's that, Uncle Tyler?* and the sexually-active twelve year old gave his incredulous but nevertheless willing niece her first insight into depravity and corruption.

By the time Anna had reached her tenth birthday she had experienced and, for the most part, enjoyed an active sex life. Tyler, always the budding entrepreneur, had quickly realized the financial rewards in touting a young and enthusiastic nymphet around the back-streets of the colliery. The fee had initially been set at a standard £1, mainly for his friends, but had risen to five pounds when one of his friend's older brother showed an active interest in bedding Horden's own *Lolita*. Anna enjoyed the attention, the presents and liked gentle and attentive males. The partnership ended when Tyler, for double the fee, introduced an older man to Anna whose predilection for oral and anal sex was the final straw for Anna. She severed all business links with her Uncle Tyler and became, basically, self-employed.

Anna first met Jackie Brown on a girls night-out in Hartlepool. Fourteen at the time and by far the youngest of the large group of females. Jackie Brown's first gushing words to the young pretty girl, *Everyone calls me Hovis.* Brown was a monster in the making, a virtual giant of a man unloved and for the most part, unwanted by his miscreant and deviant mother. Jackie could win friends and influence people by instilling terror in them but, try as he may, his success with the opposite sex, failed spectacularly. He hid his natural shyness and embarrassment with boorish and uncouth behaviour.

Hovis Brown followed the youngster like a bear smelling honey. He was besotted with Anna, *I'll do anythin' to make you happy, Anna*, he would say. So she used him like she used everyone and he became a pawn to be used at whim. She enjoyed the power and the protection that Jackie Brown gave and used it occasionally to satisfy her heinous and immoral ways. Jackie always obliged without question or conscience. After months the relationship, albeit one-sided, was still ongoing. Anna milked the big willing oaf whenever she liked, Jackie Brown was her protector and she felt safe with him, knew the deep adoration he felt for her. Sometimes, when Anna was feeling particularly generous she would succumb to his pleadings and allow the man into her bed.

His love was boundless and it had to end in tears and misery for Jackie Brown. A year into the relationship and Anna was incensed when her best friend, Emily Powlett, told her that Tommy and Tyrone Morrison (twins who worked at the colliery: Tommy named after *Tommy Roe* and Tyrone named after *Tyrone Power*) had been making their mouths go in the *Comrades*. Drunk they were and ever so vociferous about their double-act with Anna in Tyrone's new *Polo*. *Said you liked a good sandwich, Anna. Tommy was the bottom slice and Tyrone was the crust.* Emily trying to pretend she cared. *Big deal*, replied Anna, *men always exaggerate, the smaller their dicks, the bigger their boasting*. Then Emily Powlett, smirking, told a startled Anna what else they had said. It was the straw that broke the camel's back. Anna's reputation had to be protected. They could not tell blatant lies about her. *I took off my clothes got out of the bloody car and let them do what*, gasped the little actress. *Jesus Christ, men and their*

22

inflated egos. Tell me, I really want to know what lies they're spreading about me. Now Emily was smiling, couldn't help herself. *Hell, Anna, they were making it up.* Anna demanded to know anyway. She could feel a hot and uncomfortable flush covering her features, knew what was coming. She had been drunk, they had been drunk and they were having a ball. Emily continued. *They said you wanted them to pee all over you? Bollocks, I said. Anna would never do that....Would you?*

Of course Anna did not tell Jackie Brown the whole story, turned it round, adding a little twist and tug here and there. *They've been calling me, Jackie. Horrible names, because I wouldn't have anything to do with them.* Anna knew that the twins would be at the dance so she spent the night filling Jackie Brown with alcohol, begged him to protect and restore her sullied reputation. He obliged, always did, caught the youths in the toilets and battered them senseless but that wasn't enough for Anna Belling. She wanted the whole of the colliery to know what would happen if someone displeased or hurt her. *Again, Jackie, you've got to do more than bruise them, I want them hurt, Jackie. If you want our relationship to continue, Jackie, you'll cripple the bastards!*

The big fool did not know when to stop, kicked them unconscious them jumped on them for good measure. *That'll keep their gobs shut, eh, Anna.* Not a truer word said. The twins were hospitalized for weeks. Jackie was arrested, despite Anna's sworn testimony that she witnessed the twins attack her protesting boy-friend. Lost his temper big time did Jackie Brown. Tyrone was blinded in one eye and had only partial vision in the other. Tommy ended up in a wheel-chair, thanks to the giant using his neck as a trampoline. Horrific spinal injuries, that's what nailed Jackie Brown. The assault was too prolonged and too savage. He was deemed a monster, didn't help his case when he stood proudly in the dock and said that he wasn't sorry. *Tell you what Judge, I'll do it again* and *no mistake!* Then he turned, smiled and winked at a disbelieving Anna. All for Anna Belling, not a single regret, true unrequited love, he would fight the world for his Anna.

Although promising Jackie everything to waylay his natural fears at the prolonged incarceration: *I'll write every week and I'll visit fortnightly, swear, Jackie, give my word, Jackie. I'll not forget what you've done for me.* Anna immediately forgot her giant teddy-bear and moved on to pastures new. He was called Marlon McGintey, short, gaunt and with a permanent twinkle in his eye. He swept Anna off her feet within ten minutes of meeting her. Easington's *Diamond* pub: a notorious watering-hole for the colliery riff-raff was to be their first rendezvous. Marlon, a pugnacious street-fighter with an unquenchable penchant for violence and sex: W*akes me up in the morning; helps me sleep at night;* was kicking seven bells out of local hard-man Joe Danty. The pair had clashed in the toilets when the bigger and stronger man had elbowed little Marlon out of the way. *The mirror is mine, punk.* The fight was one-way as Marlon battered his opponent senseless out of the lavatory-door, Joe Danty collapsed between the visitors and Anna was immediately captivated and told him so. Minutes later and the couple were back in the men's toilets, clawing and fighting one another but only in fun.

Their union lasted a year. Anna, for once in her life, had stayed loyal to Marlon, too busy fending off the continuous amorous advances from all and sundry. Marlon couldn't, wouldn't change his philandering ways, not even for Anna. Flirted in front of her, no conscience, no qualms about his bizarre behaviour. *One life, Anna. One friggin' life.* Their rows and arguments were legendary and hurt her more than him. His philosophy, *Take it or leave it, love. This is me, full stop.* Marlon finally ended it. He had been smitten by Norma Newley, a fourteen year old beauty

24

whose mother lived in South Hetton but who was visiting her brother in Easington Colliery. Marlon's parent's lived next door to the Newley's. *Bingo*, the mismatched couple immediately became an item. Marlon was honest about his new love, never once in their full year together had he spoken to Anna in such a candid way. She was shocked. Marlon, if truth be told, was more shocked. He had found love for the first time. The couple left Marlon's home for the final time, intending to walk together to the bus-stand, turned a corner and almost collided with Jackie Brown. For one brief moment the beefy gorilla had pushed Marlon out of his path, so engrossed on finding his deceiving girl-friend. Then he stopped like he had stepped into quicksand. Wide-eyed with a mixture of shock and bewilderment and hurt, he recovered and the barracking started.

Anna imagined that Big Jackie would slaughter the smaller, punier figure but Marlon had never lost a fight in his life, would never give up, no matter how many times he was thumped to the floor, always struggled back on his feet. He had the stamina of an ox, the courage of a lion and had worn down the very best of brawlers with an utter, sometimes surreal mettle. Marlon McGintey was invincible. Five horrendous minutes later and Marlon, buzzing with heaven-sent adrenalin, stepped over the bleeding prostrate figure of Hovis Brown, laughed his way to the main street with the stunned and silent Anna by his side, forgot the bus-ride, ordered her a taxi instead and kissed a subdued Anna Belling for the last time.

Two weeks later and Anna phoned Jackie Brown. She still had her uses for the big dumb fool. *I've missed you, Jackie*. That's all it took to make the giant return to the fold.

CHAPTER FOUR

Saturday evening and the senior Bellings were contemplating whether to visit the local bingo hall or take a car-ride to Hartlepool; win junk in Horden`s *Fairworld* or take a six mile journey to the *Regal* or the *Stranton* with the chance to win serious cash. Milly Belling, 36 years old, bloated and wrinkled prematurely with a lifetime of excess, always had the final say in such matters. The old hen ruled the roost, sat hunched over the roaring open-coal fire and sucked heavily on the cigarette. Matriarch supreme, still thought she was the double of Elizabeth Taylor and she was, literally. When she was sixteen and voluptuous she could have understudied the actress for a role in *Raintree County*, twenty one years later, with a shape reminiscent of a butter-barrel, she still resembled the now swollen actress.

"Walk or bus, woman?" asked Billy, *Horden or Hartlepool?* It was minutes after six and the pick-up bus would be moving through the colliery at 6.30pm. Billy Belling would have preferred local to long-distance, his head still splitting with the previous evening's binge, mixed his bloody drinks again, always a cause of deep regret a day later.

The front door squeaked open and their eldest daughter walked into the room. Joan Belling, twenty-one, pencil-slim with a mane of black hair, flopped on the sofa, grabbed a magazine and proceeded to flick aimlessly through the pages. Moments passed and then she asked if they were going out. When she wasn't working, Joan worked on a casual basis for *Warren Fisheries*. The girl enjoyed the occasional night out with her parents. Two weeks ago she had scooped £300 in a jackpot and shared the money equally between the three of them. Different as chalk and cheese when compared to her two flighty, feisty sisters. Any winnings falling in their laps would have disappeared straight into their purses. Joan, head and shoulders taller than her sisters, was definitely cloned from the building-bricks of father Billy. Quiet, ponderous and mature, she shunned the night-life frequented by her two siblings, preferring television to tequila, books to booze, bingo to binge-drinking - hence the single status of the girl. She had tried the clubs and pubs but found them boring, the men especially were too loud, too full of drink and their brains between their legs. Joan had shunned that life for years.

Joan liked Jackie Brown, could see past the brash arrogance of the man, all the posing and preening tattooed over his enormous frame was an act. He was a big soft teddy-bear. Trouble with Jackie was Anna. Anna pulled and played with the heart-strings of the human teddy-bear. Jackie Brown adored her, told Joan one night when Anna had done her usual vanishing act and left him distraught with worry. *What shall I do, Joan, she's got me head in bits*! How could Joan answer honestly? *You're being used, Jackie, she's my sister but she'll chase anything in trousers*. Joan could neither hurt him or her sister. *Go home Jackie, love. I'll tell her to phone you when she gets back.* It was almost a year since Anna had booted him out of their home. Jackie was back living in Hartlepool, heard he was working on the taxis. Poor Jackie Brown could not see the evil manipulator that was her little sister, so besotted he'd gone to jail for her and came out wanting more. Joan liked Jackie Brown, she wished he liked her.

"Dad?" reminded Joan, it was 6.15pm and if they were going to the town then they needed to leave now.

"Ask your Ma, love," replied Billy and moved to the kitchen and found a box of *Headex*. Swallowed three for luck. *Never again,* he moaned, rubbing at his throbbing skull, *never again*!

"Horden, our Joan," decided Milly Belling, "make a cuppa, love?" and watched as her eldest waltzed into the kitchen. "And a *Cadbury's Dairy Milk*, Joan, there's a giant bar in the pantry, we'll share it, eh?"

Joan glanced at her father and smiled and Billy shook his head, his wife had some appetite. Her daily intake could easily feed a village of *Biafrans* for a week and as for sharing the *Dairy Milk*, chance would be a fine thing. *We'll share the ginger-snaps, Joan,* said the man, *let's not upset your mother?* Like clock-work was Milly, give it twenty minutes when she was lifting her bulk off the chair and finding her coat she'd rattle off the same old tune. *D'you think me backside is getting bigger, Bill, tell me the truth, now?* Once and only once, he'd told her her arse was enormous and he was banished to the single bed for a week, made his own meals too. *Don't be so selfish, Bill, how d'you expect me to cook for you when I'm tryin' Weight-Watchers just for you?*

9.45pm and they'd sweated on three separate occasions. Out of luck, won nothing but enjoyed themselves because the chat had been good. Billy, feeling much better since the headache tablets had kicked-in, suggested a drink in the *Trust*. The pub was across the road from the bingo-hall, *Just the one, love?* Milly was agreeable so the trio wandered into the rear of the public-house. The lounge was always quiet. One drink and then across the back-street to *Warren Fisheries* for their well-earned supper. If Doug Mountjoy was having a shift off, then Brenda Flecker, chief fryer and good friend of Joan, would slip then some freebies.

Joan went to the counter and waited patiently. The young barmaid was in the bar. From where Joan was standing she could see one half of the other, more crowded room, recognized the two men deep in conversation standing close to the counter. Hovis Brown stood out like a sore thumb. *Jack the Giant*, she smiled. The man with him was Ryan Dimonti, a nasty vindictive man with a sordid reputation to boot, a criminal and low-life drug-peddler shunned by most law-abiding folk. Dimonti, an ex-miner, had hit the jackpot when the N.C.B. had believed his lies about his damaged spine. Fooled the Coal Company and a host of gullible doctors eight years previously, received a whopper payout, plus a guaranteed weekly benefit cheque that helped him jump-start his criminal career. The barmaid returned and Joan ordered the drinks. She kept looking at the big man, hoping to catch his eye. Jackie Brown was too interested in the instructions from the smaller man. A little miffed, she turned and started carrying the tray of drinks to her waiting parents, didn't see the huge tousled head turn and follow her from the bar until she disappeared, didn't see the sparkle in his big brown eyes as he recognized the girl.

"Anna's Jackie is in the bar," said Joan, placing the drinks on the small scratched table. *Double-Maxim* and a packet of *Golden-Wonder* crisps for Milly, a pint of *Newcastle Best* for Billy and a *Cider and Green Ginger* for her, returned the tray to the counter and looked quickly into the bar. Jackie Brown had disappeared. Ryan Dimonti guzzled greedily at his pint, saw the girl staring and his eyes feasted on Joan. She ignored him and returned to her parents, wondered where Jackie Brown had gone.

"Hovis Brown, you say, our Joan?" asked Bill, his glass already half-empty, "canny lad is Hovis." He pondered awhile then added, "Wonder why he left our Anna? They seemed to get on well."

"Bad influence," mouthed Milly, her mouth full of sodden crisps. "Hovis Brown, stupid name for a stupid fella, if you ask me!"

"He didn't leave," said a defensive Joan, "our Anna was seein' Jerome Briggs but Jerome was scared that Jackie would find out about them. Thought Jackie would do the same to him as he did to Tyrone and Tommy Morrison. Joan remembered the conversation with her younger sister.

Honest to Christ, Joan. Jackie was walking through the back door and I was pushing Jerome out of the front. He was stark naked, runnin' up the street without a stitch on. Joan couldn't see the humour, only saw the deceit. *God, Anna, if he finds out!*

"He was okay, was Hovis," said Billy, finished his drink. "One for the road, girls?"

"Whiskey and lemonade," said Milly. She had hardly touched her beer.

"I'm fine, Dad," said Joan, "this will do me for tonight."

The man sauntered to the counter. In the bar, the juke-box spluttered into life: Don Mclean's *Crying*. Billy Belling was transported back to 1961, young again, newly married and his head still in the clouds of passion and promise turned, shouted to his wife. "Listen, Milly, our song," added whimsically, "can't beat Roy Orbison, eh?" He was starting to enjoy himself, decided to order a whiskey-chaser.

"I liked Jackie Brown," confessed Joan.

"He was an arse, our Joan," retorted the mother bluntly, "big and soft, let our Anna do what she wanted, putty for brains!"

"He cared about Anna and she took advantage of him."

"Tied to her apron-strings," insisted Milly Belling, "that's no good for a relationship."

Joan drank from her glass, too polite to argue with her mother. *Just like dad,* she thought.

CHAPTER FIVE

Ryan Dimonti, 35 years old, average height, average looks, didn't stand out in a crowd dress-wise, however, Dimonti was a trend-setter, bought the right newspapers and the glossy magazines, looked the part as *Mister Cool*. Could have passed as a hip bank manager or a trendy civil-servant, *young professional* stamped across his smooth forehead. The hair-style let him down. Unorthodox could best describe the wild, healthy chocolate-coloured straw that blossomed from his skull, neither wanted nor enjoyed. It was the cross the criminal had to bear, no matter the gel or the dressing, the hair stayed seemingly uncultivated and feral. *Is that a crew-cut, Ryan,* they would mock when he was a youth, *a buzz-cut?* All his pals were exact clones of *Elvis* or *Cliff* and he was forever an overblown version of *Joe Brown.* And when the fashion fast-forwarded to *Mod, Rocker, Romantic* or *Punk* his friends and acquaintances moved and adapted, their prerogative only, Dimonti, when it came to hair-styles, was forever stuck in the *fifties.*

He was always known for his fiery temperament, had the occasional rumble and tumble to which most teenagers are prone, the odd disagreement when he was at the colliery. There were other times when awful acts were attributed to Ryan, acts of mayhem that somehow were accredited to the youth. Rumours, innuendos, nothing more. For the most part, Ryan Dimonti was one of the crowd, more boisterous than some but essentially more interested in the good things in life. A teenager, burning incessantly with a heady mix of hormones and adrenalin of the natural kind, living the dreams and hopes of a normal healthy youth.

That eventful week-end saw a whole bunch of youngsters buzzing with promise and feigned prowess, visiting Sunderland's finest haunts. Beatlemania was rampant. Everyone of a certain age had swapped the greased-back look for the more natural mop sported by the newest Messiahs of pop, the *basin-cut* was back with a vengeance, the Mississippi swamped by the Mersey. Everyone tried to emulate *John, Paul, George* or *Ringo*. Ryan Dimonti, still impersonating someone who'd escaped from a chain-gang or who was having a break from scaring the crows, was at the bar ordering drinks, trying hard not to look at the huge mirror that filled the wall behind the bar. He was surrounded by half a dozen trendies, *Liverpool replicas,* who immediately began barracking and ridiculing him. His friends watched with a growing tension. They were not trouble-makers. Outgunned in age and height, they stood and prayed for the hostility and the opposition to dissipate. They could not see Ryan Dimonti, hidden by the size and bulk of the aggressors.

Someone pushed Ryan, not strongly, more a nudge and the youth responded with more of the same, already pleading for peace, trying not to show fear. *I'm not after trouble, pal,* he pleaded, eyeing up the competition. *Just let it go, man!* The odds were not in his favour so his temper, for once, was held in check. Another push, more aggressive this time, sent Ryan stumbling into others in the group, a fist caught him on the back of the head and the youth knew he had to do something before he was thrashed. Lunging along the wide expanse of the counter, he shoved for all he was worth, shrieked as if were a crazy man, stumbling and flaying at all and sundry. He rocketed forwards, into the biggest and meanest of the gang. Luck was on his side. As he hurled himself at the brute, his foot landed squarely on his opponent's shoe, trapping him and making it nigh impossible to move or react to the charging youth. Down he went like a ton of screaming bricks with the frenzied and howling Dimonti clinging to his chest. The bigger man's head made heavy contact with the trendy steel tubing that skirted the entire length of the bar-counter, installed primarily as a foot-rest, it became a heaven-sent head-rest and knocked the aggressor out cold. All hell broke lose as two enormous bouncers suddenly appeared and proceeded to scatter the gang. Only Ryan Dimonti, still on top of the unconscious brute, was left at the bar. The dazed youth was dragged to his feet, threatened and frog-marched out of the pub and past a disbelieving gaggle of friends. Ryan Dimonti's reputation was made, he had beaten a giant of a man, knocked him clean out. *Did you see that punch?* said one of his pals. *Brilliant,* said another. *He was like Roberto Duran,* said another. *Marvin Hagler,* cried someone. It did not seem to matter that no-one had actually witnessed the scuffle, only the outcome was relevant. Ryan Dimonti, still shaking from the melee, wisely kept his opinions to himself.

The word quickly spread through the colliery. *Don't mess with Dimonti!*

He left the Trust at 10.30. The *Volvo* was parked near to the front-door of the pub on the heavy bend of the main road, close to the traffic-lights. Parked awkwardly on purpose, all show, let people know he was about; even had the personalized number plates: *RD 500.* That's what the game was all about. He had respect from both sides of the law. It was all about clout. When to use it, when to broadcast it because nothing worked better than fear. He had used it periodically over the years. His reputation had grown and grown out of all proportion, even he was amazed at the stories he'd heard about himself, so naturally he milked it for all it was worth. Years ago, younger, fitter, he had played down his occasional mishaps, his dark deeds, didn't want the reputation that was part and parcel of the wicked game. So different now, built his own bridges. *Called me a thief,* boasted the man, *gave him a chance to apologise, when he didn't, I fire-bombed his car! Cool or what? The loudmouth bought another so I cut the brakes, wrecked his motor and a United bus. He moved outa the district!* The stories were boundless, fantastic and horrific. *I was minding my own business, just wanting the shift to finish. Can you believe it, down the pit and whitewashing? Said I was a trouble-maker so I was working on my own, then this bloke, bigger and older than me, who was built like a tank, picks on me. Naturally I defended myself. The under-manager stopped the fight, sent me out of the pit, said I'd never work at the mine again. Two weeks and the union got me my job back. The other man never worked again.* Ryan Dimonti stoking the fires of intrigue and conspiracy, if it helped enhance his sordid reputation to his own selfish ends then so be it. People started looking at the man in a different way, gained respect and deference from some and from others, admiration and fear.

Earlier, he had sent his very own big man to East Durham. *Who the hell is this Primo Carnera, Mr. Dimonti? Everyone calls me Hovis or Big Jack.* Dumb wasn't the word for Jackie Brown, never heard of Consett. *Bloody biggest steel works in the North-East used to be there, Primo. Drive west, straight past Durham.* Waste of time trying to educate the gorilla, ended up drawing a street-map. *Don't knock on the door, man. Walk in, hit him hard and then tell him who sent you!* Nicky Thompson, a piddling of a middleman, was becoming an embarrassment by withholding money from Ryan Dimonti. *Do as I say, Primo and there'll be a big bonus for you.*

The *Volvo* was driven to the Crossroads Estate on the outskirts of Horden. Dimonti was no fool, his car was his only extravagance and even that had been purchased from a bent motor-dealer who doctored the buying price way below the book-value. It paid to cover your mucky tracks. The house, a council-semi, was situated in McGuiness Avenue. Ryan was looking forward to a playful few hours with two of the young and very adventurous Belling sisters.

The things that money could buy.

He drove along the coastal road and pulled up outside of the *Bell* pub, saw the two girls waiting, huddled in the doorway. Ryan Diminti sounded the horn.

"Why can't we both stay all night, Anna?" whined the oldest sister.

"Because he's mine, Milly!" spat the shorter female. "He just needs a bit of persuading is all!" She began to walk slowly and provocatively towards the waiting vehicle.

Milly caught up with her, too close to the car to talk normally she whispered, "What about Corky? You're livin' with him."

Cornelius Robinson, a 20 year old collier was Anna's latest beau. They'd been living together at the Handley Street address since Hovis Brown had been evicted, worshiped her enough to be blinded by her lies and deceit. *Corky, give it a rest will you. It was late when we got back from the nightclub. I slept in our Milly's bed. Of course Ma didn't mind, why should she, I'm her bloody daughter!*

Anna stopped and grabbed at her sister. Despite her age and height advantage, Milly was not in the same league when it came to violence and vindictiveness. "You're pregnant, shall I tell Albert Squires about tonight?"

"Okay," spluttered Milly, "sorry I spoke!"

"Might tell him who the real daddy is, eh, Milly?"

"Let me go, Anna... Ryan is watching!"

Consett.

At 11.10pm Hovis Brown drove the Vauxhall *Cavalier* slowly along the darkened street. Minutes earlier he had parked, checked the number of the first house, had to be certain that he entered the correct home. Started driving and counting, half-way along and he had reached his destination. *Show-time*, he thought. The giant clambered out of the battered motor, hesitated momentarily then reached for his baseball-bat hidden in the sleeve of his coat. Hovis took deep breaths to hide his growing nerves then walked purposefully along the garden-path.

The house was unlocked. Gingerly he eased open the door and stepped into the dim room. Somewhere in the home a television was playing at full volume. The intruder inched forward and reached another door, the noise of the television-set blared out *Thaw* and *Waterman*. *Minder*! Another deep breath and Hovis Brown wrenched open the interior-door then stopped dead in his tracks. Either side of the flickering screen sat an old couple, the man wearing an enormous hearing-aid, sat sprawled over the large and ancient arm-chair his eyes glued to the antics of the comic cops, deaf as Quasimodo, the volume horrendous: *Flying-Squad, mate, put down the gun*! John Thaw playing *John Wayne*. The crone opposite casually placed her knitting needles on her lap, had the audacity to smile a warm toothless smile at the statuesque and extremely confused thug. Leaning forward she fiddled with the volume-control until the shrieking turned to whispers.

"What the hell yer playin' at woman!" bellowed the husband as he too leaned forward to re-adjust the set, only then did he notice the stranger gaping at them.

"Yer'll be wantin' Nicky Thompson?" smiled the old woman.

Hovis nodded, sick to his stomach, he could see all of his money and the bonus, staying in the pockets of Mr. Dimonti.

"Odds and evens, love," said Ada Brewer. "Our side of the street is odd numbers; opposite side of the road is even numbers." She glanced at the stern wizened face of her partner, repeated the information, spoke slowly and carefully so that he could easily read her lips.

The old man nodded at his wife and then acknowledged the brute. "Aye, she's right!" Henry Brewer focused on his wife, "get some tea made, woman, we've got guests."

Struggling to her stocking-feet, the pensioner hobbled towards Hovis Brown. She was without fear as she said casually, "Yer'll stay for a cuppa, pet," and without waiting for an answer squeezed past the criminal and entered the kitchen.

Minutes later and the criminal was sitting uncomfortably on the threadbare and dilapidated sofa, his huge backside swallowed in the knackered mounds of material and almost touching the carpet underneath, knees up to his chest. The small cup of tea acutely and uncomfortably perched in one hand (due entirely to the wedged baseball-bat up his jacket-sleeve) and the spam-sandwich perilously positioned on the chair-arm, listening to Ada Brewer as she explained the situation. It was a regular occurrence apparently. Nicky's customers, like Hovis, totally confused with the illogic use of numbers, would call on the old couple. Immune and unabashed at the nefarious trade in drugs, cigarettes and alcohol, the couple had, only occasionally, taken stock from shady characters. *Middle of the night sometimes, love, Nicky has flown the coop. Will you pass this stuff to him when he returns?* The couple, for the odd gift, would readily comply with the requests. *Of course, petal, young Nicky is in France for a few days. Booze-run, you know. Leave it with us.*

Then the good news was told to Hovis Brown. Nicky Thompson was not away on his travels, he was local and they had spoken to him that same evening. The junior drug-dealer was dealing in the area: Crook, Wolsingham and Quebec and would be home at midnight. Hovis tried to excuse himself, would sit out the remainder of the night in his car. He thanked the pensioners for their hospitality and kindness. His backside was numb, his arm, with wooden accomplishment, was stinging with *pins-and needles,* the man needed to walk, move and exercise his aching joints.

He was unceremoniously overruled and he sat, glum-faced, with a growing migraine and stared morosely at the howling screen.

2.00am and Jackie Brown drove slowly into the large estate on the outskirts of Horden Colliery. He had a large wad of cash, courtesy of the drug-dealer, Nicky Thompson. The young punk had offered no resistance after the big man had broken his nose, the aggression over in minutes with a warning of more broken bones if the cretin was ever late with his payments to Mr. Dimonti. Jackie Brown was driving home, happy with his lot, easy money and a bonus, couldn't remember though whether or not he had to call on his boss tonight or tomorrow: memory like a sieve. *Middle of the night, what to do?* He decided to drive to Diminti's house and, if the lights were on, he would knock on the door. Softly.

He reached the home, it was in darkness. Cursing, Jackie Brown decided he would hold the debt-money overnight, crunched at the gears and was just about to pull away when he saw the female hurry from the place. His door was wrenched open, it was Milly Belling, Anna's sister.

"Hovis!" she gasped, "thought you were my taxi."

"Milly!" muttered a surprised Jackie Brown. "What yer doin' at Mr. Dimonti's?"

Milly clambered in the car. The big buffoon could chauffeur her home, would save on the taxi-fare. "Could ask the same?"

"Done a job for Mr. Dimonti, you know?" said Jackie as he drove along the deserted streets, "just finished. I'm not sure if he wants me to call tonight or tomorrow?"

Milly nodded, stared ahead, weary with the demands and idiosyncrasies and vigour of Ryan Dimonti, she wanted to sleep so bad. Her whole body ached.

"You and Mr. Dimonti?" quizzed the enforcer, "you two an item, or what?"

Wish I could tell you the bloody truth, Hovis, wouldn't there be fireworks, eh? The woman nodded sullenly, conversation was the last thing on her mind. "Something like that, Hovis, nothing serious."

The journey was completed in silence, both deep in their own thoughts. The vehicle squeaked to a halt outside the terraced house in the heart of the colliery and Milly dragged her body out of the car, her head thumping fearfully with the effects of alcohol. She had been plied with drinks at the Dimonti home. *Drink as much as you want girls, it's free.* She thanked Jackie Brown for his kindness and was about to take her leave.

"How's Anna?" asked the driver leaning across the expanse of the passenger-seat and staring intently at the girl. He couldn't stop himself asking after her, missed her so much that he cared little about any embarrassing rebuke that could come his way.

"Hovis, love," said Milly surprisingly sweetly as she rose above her self-inflicted wretchedness, "don't waste your time thinking about Anna."

Jackie Brown stiffened involuntarily, tried to smile but the result only added to the facial distortion.

"Anna is living with the same fella, love." She felt the discomfort radiating from the seated figure, added hesitantly, "Whether or not she stays with Corky Robinson is anyone's guess. You know Anna. She soon gets sick. Her and Corky are on a knife-edge at the moment, who knows, eh?" *How do you make a fool change his mind? Tell him the truth about Anna? She's a little whore, Jackie. Move on, eh?*

"Thanks, Milly," said the man.

"Don't build up hope, Hovis, pet, best you forget Anna. She's not the one for you. She'll never settle down, will Anna." The girl turned and walked away.

Jackie Brown drove his car through the empty streets, slowed to walking pace as the house was reached, Handley Street. Looked up at the bedroom-window and imagined Anna asleep, Anna asleep next to her Corky. Jackie shivered with discomfort. Revving at the motor, the man headed for the coast road. He would go home, good old Hartlepool, Mecca of the North-East and he smiled grimly.

It started to rain, slowly at first then grew in momentum and ferocity as it battered at the vehicle, suited his mood. *Bring it on*, he thought. *Bring it on.*

CHAPTER SIX

Anna lay stiff and uncomfortable in her bed. It was 6.00am. She had struggled into her home barely 10 minutes earlier. Corky Robinson was due in from the colliery soon. She had been unable to cook his breakfast, couldn't care less, felt feverish and light-headed. The young woman was wearing pyjamas, unusual but very necessary this day; her breasts were splattered with bruising and love-bites, her rump still smarting from his powerful slaps. Ryan Dimonti was a devil and a rogue. Old enough to be her father, he was everything she wanted in a man, strong and powerful, bursting with a charismatic, almost bestial quality. A determined, resourceful and driven individual, blinkered in his search for power and money, dripping with a leathered resilience that came from deep within his psyche.

She had never met anyone quite like him. When Anna was in his company she felt protected, blanketed and secure with his ways. It reminded Anna of Jackie Brown. Around the brutish but loveable giant she had always felt cosseted and sheltered but protection alone was not enough for the young and scheming girl. She craved attention, had all her life and not just the attention that followed her beauty. That was a temporary affair to be used and discarded at will. Men, for the most part, were weak transparent people, selfish and driven by their hungers and desire to say anything in order to satiate their craving. The attention for which she ached came from ultimate power, strength enough to sway and demand subservience, fear was the key, fear and money and Ryan Dimonti had it all.

The downstairs-door was opened noisily. It was Cornelius. *You're called what? Corky, like the bloody cat?* Not the brightest of sparks was Corky. *Named after my granddad, Cornelius Robinson. Ma thought Corky would get me mentioned in his will.* The girl had immediately

41

relented with her barracking. He was a handsome lad, good in bed, better than Jackie Brown, anyone was better than Jackie Brown. *You're smothering me, Jackie, for Christ's sake!* He did indeed receive a windfall, smaller than Anna was hoping for but enough to keep her smiling. *Corky, love, we'll buy a car next year, let's enjoy ourselves while we can?* More of a stop-gap for Anna. He would eventually have to go, trouble was, he was going to be more of an obstacle than Jackie Brown. Say jump to Jackie Brown and he jumped. Corky, although besotted with the female, was occasionally an obstinate and unbending young man. She grimaced; something would turn up, only a matter of time before Corky was kicked into touch.

"Anna, you sleep in?" Corky sounded rattled. Who could blame him, seven hours underground and no meal waiting on the table.

Sleep would be nice, thought Anna, closed her eyes and pulled the duvet up to her nose, knowing the man expected breakfast. *Whistle for it, Corky.*

The young collier hurried up the stairs and entered the small bedroom, his hair still damp and limp from the pit-showers. He moved to the bed, touched the prostrate figure. *Slept in again?* Corky smiled as he traced gently at the soft inviting outline, his immature head bouncing with hormones, directing him to a quick and sweaty dose of impromptu activity with the girl.

She heard the familiar rustle as the young miner fumbled at his clothing, said steely, "Forget it, Corky, I'm full of cold and I've just started my periods."

"Started?" *Started falling asleep, started waking up*, he thought, who cared about a little of the crimson stuff.

"Periods, Corky," she turned her back on him "and I'm heavy!"

The frustration boiled over, twenty years old and bursting with passion. "Since when has that stopped us?" His dummy was lost and he was in a tantrum, "you always say you like it when you bleed!" He pulled at the bed-cover; saw the lovely and sensuous shape of her back-side drawing him like a lonely siren. Anna was wearing pajamas, she hardly ever wore clothes for bed, crunched his face in annoyance, thinking: *Must be ill.*

She thought about her bruised body. *Jesus Christ,* thought Anna, creeping with fear, twisting her head and feigning illness she uttered, "Sorry, pet but I feel like shit, been up all night." *And that's the truth.* "Haven't had any sleep."

Corky relented, thinking himself selfish. He would make her a cup of tea, perhaps refresh her. "Sorry Anna, I'll put the kettle on, make you feel better."

"Thanks Corky," she whispered, "you're a treasure," she closed her eyes and fell immediately to sleep................

She was nine years old and Mr. Tomkins was shouting at her again, scolding her for not paying attention in the lesson. Anna had dozed off and her wheezing had caught the young teacher's attention. She didn't like Mr. Tomkins, he was always shouting at the pupils. He always seemed angry, at war with the class, with life and with himself. He was old but not as old as Miss Pearce who had white hair and knobbly, ugly fingers. Mr. Tomkins had wild and crinkly hair the colour of sand and a beard. He was the only man she had seen with a full beard. Mr. Brown - Uncle Tyler had said he was called Mr. Brown but she knew he was lying because last week Mr. Brown had been Mr. Smith - also had a beard but it was trim and neat and tickled when he tried to kiss her. The teacher reminded Anna of a pirate from Never-Never Land. When he had first arrived at her school he had an eye-patch. He looked frightening. Most of the time the whole class behaved for Mr. Tomkins. It was the untamed sight of the beard and the eye-patch, fearsome to look at. He shouted all the time, gnashed his big teeth and fumed at everyone. Shaun Lockey called him Captain Hook, but only in the playground.

The first time he came to the lesson without the eye-patch every pupil stared at the puckered and crimson features around the new eye. When Mr. Tomkins looked directly at you he looked okay, agitated but okay. Anna knew something was wrong though. When the tutor glanced at an angle it was obvious that the new eye was not working properly. He became wall-eyed or cross-eyed depending on his stance because the new eye stared straight ahead. Albert Newcome, the class clown, was dragged unceremoniously out of the classroom and to the headmaster's office. *Is that a glass eye, sir?* Said it too loud, stared too long, a simple question from a curious, fatuous ten year old. First and only time anyone asked about Mr. Tomkins's glass eye.

She almost wet her knickers, fast asleep one minute and the next being dragged to the front to the class. Little cretin! Mr. Tomkins shrieked. My lessons are so boring that you think you can sleep through them?She was pushed into a corner at the front of the room, told to face the wall, touch the cold wall with her head and not to move a muscle. She did and closed her eyes again. Anna had been out with her Uncle Tyler until very late. He had taken her to the man's home again. They had been visiting the fellow's house for weeks now. Mr. Brown's house - who only a week ago had been Mr. Smith, but Anna kept quiet, it didn't matter. He was so nice to Anna. When Uncle Tyler had left her alone in the house Mr. Brown had spent some time just talking to her. He seemed to live on his own and yet the home was filled with bric-a-brac, normal to a family home – photographs and plaques littered a large sideboard. Family pictures: a man and his wife in one large photograph. Another showed the same couple with a small boy. A portrait on the wall above the television showed a grinning boy dressed in football clothes holding the silver cup aloft. Mr. Brown wouldn't talk about himself or his missing family, talked incessantly to the little tot, but only about her.

Sometimes they would sit together on the settee and the man would simply cuddle her. Sometimes he kissed her, but only if she let him. He was ever so gentle with Anna. There was always plenty to eat and drink, sweets and chocolates and candy. And drink too. Sometimes the drink was sickly and too sweet and she seemed to drift away but it was a nice feeling. She felt so relaxed and cocooned with the man. Mr. Brown, unknown to Uncle Tyler, would always put money in her coat-pocket. That's for you, honey. Don't tell Tyler. He's already been paid. She enjoyed bath-time the best, all the hot water and the mountain of bubbles. Mr. Brown was so gentle when he washed her. When he dried her he dabbed and pattered at her thin body with the large and soft towel, like she was a porcelain-doll. Precious. Later, lying spread-eagled and relaxed in front of the roaring fire, the man would sprinkle talcum-powder over her like gold-dust, his hands soft and caressing. Mr. Brown was so nice, had even purchased her a lovely nightgown, all patterned with silver and shine. Anna loved the nightgown. It always ended with the pair of them lying together across the sofa. *Close your eyes, Anna, promise you won't open them until I say* and the little girl would relax as her nightgown was carefully lifted. He never physically consummated the act, satisfied in his own sick and perverted way to simply stare at the beautiful and inviting sight. Anna would listen as he softly moaned and moved, young eyes opened like slits, enjoying the mad spectacle.............

"Anna? Anna?" whispered Corky Robinson. He stood over her sleeping wheezing body, cup of tea in one hand; the other hand caressing the moist locks. She did not stir.

The young collier relented, walked slowly and silently out of the bedroom, down the stairs thinking: *No food in the house. Damn and blast, Anna!* None to speak of as such but there was bread and margarine, a jar of jam and a tin of Heinz beans. His features lit up, he'd have a hot breakfast after all: beans on toast, yes, beans on toast and some *McVities's* half coated and perhaps, if he were lucky, he'd have Anna later. He grinned and moved to the dinky kitchen.

Later that day.

Joan gave the gentlest of taps on the door and stepped in to the kitchen. "Anna, are you in?"

"In here," came the dazed voice.

The oldest sister stepped into the living-room; observed Anna spread-eagled over the sofa, draped in her dressing-gown, half-asleep, the television blared to itself. "Hi, Anna," said Joan, "everything okay?"

"What a night," gasped Anna and she struggled to an upright position, she was still wearing pajamas.

"Corky?"

"Naw, stupid, Corky was in night-shift."

Joan smiled benignly, "I'll make some tea."

"Aspirins, Joan," asked the youngest, "you got any?"

"I'll put the kettle on and call in Mayhills." The grocery shop was minutes away, "Give me a few minutes, Anna."

"Thanks, Joan, you're a Godsend."

Ten minutes, two cups of tea, toast and four paracetamols later and Anna Belling was almost her old self.

"You've forgotten?"

Anna sipped at the sweet tea, shook her waxen head in puzzlement.

"Nana Belling?"

46

Alice Belling, their Dad's mum and a widow, lived in Easinton Colliery. Not in the best of health, Alice looked forward to the weekly visit from her grandchildren. Joan called several times a week, the other girls visited when and if the mood took them.

"Couldn't face all that cleaning, Joan," moaned Anna.

Joan followed, glum-faced and resigned. "Anna," she said diplomatically, "you don't do any work at Nan's. You chat to her and watch the television. I do all the cleaning and the shopping."

"Easington," moaned Anna as she stretched out, "got to wait for a bus, sometimes walk up the hill from the *Diamond*. Couple hour's gossip and then all the way back, it's hard work, Joan." She glanced at the clock. "It's almost one-o-clock now and Corky will be out of bed by four... want his tea."

"Please, Anna, Nana always asks about you."

An hour later.

Joan missed the bus that would have taken her all the way to *Home Hill Estate*. She walked quickly from the *Diamond* corner up the long sweeping incline towards the estate. The sun shone but the wind whipped and tormented her. Something caught her eye and Joan glanced towards the graveyard. A rolling wreath, ribbons fluttering wildly as the green wheel burst from the bleakness of the grey and black headstones and made its escape. An old woman, propped on the edge of the council bench close to the obelisk with headscarf tightly bound around her wrinkled features, watched the macabre sight. The wreath started dipping and weaving as it eased from the gale, an exhausted spinning-top and its journey almost over as it struggled to the pensioner's side. Joan slowed her pace, mesmerized and watched as the pensioner leaned forward and grasped the garland and read the inscription. The old woman struggled to unsteady feet and, holding the prize, shuffled into the maze of headstones looking for its home. There she stood statuesque and sentry-like, the wreath cradled to her chest as she stared at the mound of clay.

"Let me think, Joan," said the wizened figure, almost lost in the decrepit depths of the arm-chair. "Who's buried today?" and she studied the roaring flames in the grate, her thin lips mulching and chewing over the question, slapped her palms together gleefully and muttered, "Luke Parkin, the old bugger!"

"Know him Nana?"

"Older than me," she cackled, "same age as your granddad, bless his soul, same class at school." She grinned mischievously at her granddaughter adding, "Used to fancy me, that's why your granddad never liked him."

"Memories, Nan?"

"Memories indeed, pet, that's all I've got left."

"Don't talk like that, Nana," said Joan, "you've got us."

"Only you put yerself out, pet... let's be honest."

"Milly is at the ante-natal and Anna is ill," answered Joan.

"What a family," sighed the pensioner, "One pregnant and still at home, the other living with someone and not married. Back to front, our Joan." She grabbed the poker and stabbed at the burning coals. "No one on the horizon, Joan?"

"I'm only twenty-one, Nan, there's plenty of time for me."

"Billy Butlin still asks after you."

John Butlin, twenty-five, a bus-driver and Alice Belling's unmarried neighbour, liked Joan. They had dated over the past year and although John clearly wanted to take the relationship further, Joan was reluctant. There was no spark or tingle, when she was with him. It would have been easy to follow her Grandmother's advice: *Got to like a man first, the love comes later, Joan. Love at first sight is for fairy-tales.* Joan knew different. The first time she had seen Jackie Brown she felt a surge of emotion she had never felt in her life, couldn't explain it in a thousand years. Big as a bear with features hewn from granite, he was no matinee idol. He was besotted with her sister, Anna and worshiped her so he was untouchable to Joan, out of reach, even though Anna had discarded him. Joan knew the love he felt for her wayward and wild sister. She never told anyone how she felt, too embarrassed and too shy.

She changed the subject. "Nan, the pantry is empty and the fridge is low. Think I should shop first then clean, okay?"

"Billy is in, Joan," chuckled the old woman. "He's on six till two this week. Shall I phone next door ask him if he wants a bite to eat?"

Joan pulled on her coat, "I'm going to the co-op, Nan, don't you dare ask John in for tea!"

"Your loss, pet," answered Alice, shaking her head. She remembered the prescription, "call in the doctor's, Joan, I'm out of Valium again."

"Nan, you don't need them!"

"It's a look out for me, pet," whined Alice pathetically. "The surgery is always full, it's the only time I see folk. If my back wasn't bad I'd be down myself."

"You've got boxes of the stuff!"

"Never know when I'll need them, pet!" her voice rose in anger. "Wait till you're old, Joan, it's hell!"

"I'll get your tablets, Nan."

CHAPTER SEVEN

Hovis Brown, awake for minutes and still in a fog of fatigue, stood lethargically next to the ancient cooker. The only working ring on the old appliance was blasting unmercifully at the putrid frying-pan, the bacon and eggs, black-pudding and beans were waiting to be tossed into the cooking-pot. He gazed momentarily at the solitary side window ignoring the accumulated muck and grime that infested the entire pane. In one filthy corner a fly buzzed like a kettle as a spider spun its liquid steel around its protesting body, wrapped like a mummy in seconds. In the distance, *Hartlepool Bay*, bleak and untiring, waves and froth were being whisked and twirled in the cold strong wind. *South Crescent, the Headland*, his home, a converted and ancient building bulging with seedy flatlets overlooking the ocean, *Dickens* would have been proud. This was Jackie's home since he'd left Horden.

The telephone shook away his stupor, switching off the hissing gas jet he grabbed the receiver.

"Hey!" said the caller, all aggression and bite.

"Mr. Dimonti?"

"Who else, man," Ryan smarting to hear the news.

"Called last night, Mr. Dimonti," spluttered the buffoon, "you were in bed, well, Milly Belling said you were in bed and that I should take her home. She'd ordered a taxi but when I showed...."

"Steady on, Primo!" stamped the man.

"Sorry, Mr. Dimonti." Seconds of silence. *Does he want me to speak or stay quiet? Maybe I should say somethin'?* "I got your money, Mr. Dimonti, plus some extra." *Don't call me Primo!*

"And what?"

"Pardon, Mr. Dimonti?" *Scares the fuck outa me!*

"And when do I see my money, Primo, you gonna store it or fetch it?"

"One hour, Mr. Dimonti, if that's okay with you?"

"Okay, man."

"Right then," Jackie said about to put down the phone.

"Hey," said the voice on the line, "you done well, man!" *Click*.

Jackie Brown turned the gas-ring back on, found the *Swan-Vestas*, struck the last match in the box and finished the fry-up, he was ravished. He approached the small creaky table, pushed aside milk-bottles and ash-trays and the half-empty *Heinz* ketchup bottle. Turned to a clean page of the *Hartlepool Mail* and used it as a cover. Knife and fork, chipped cup and large dinner-plate were placed on the crisp, clean newsprint. He ate in silence, struggling to read again the days-old news from the paper, rest half an hour and then he'd call on Mr. Dimonti. He pulled out a fag; the packet said *German*, cheap as muck and tasted like manure, grabbed at the empty box of matches and cursed loudly. The gas fire was manipulated and the flame spluttered then grew as the bar ignited, the cigarette was pushed gingerly through the wired grid and touched the naked flame.

Jackie Brown looked around at the bed-sit, felt ashamed. He'd inherited the decrepit flat, plus junk-yard contents, months ago from some burnt-out ageing hippy. Cursing his lazy mother all his life and he was as bad, worse even. The bed, permanently unmade, sheets in need of a boil, months without *Ariel* or *Daz* and they were so stiff with accumulated sweat that they could stand on their own. No wonder he was struggling with relationships. One large infested room with the solitary door to the ancient bathroom and lavatory, who could ask for more, nothing had really changed in his life. *Hey, girls, you want, I'll switch on the 12 inch black and white. Music, that's an original Dansette: circa 1964. The records, who else, The Chiffons, The Ronettes.... The best of Berry Gordy*! Jackie

Brown had found *The Motown Story* in the filthy toilet. Music to dump by? He'd read it cover to cover, *Oh, the Shenanigans from Detroit, Eastenders with American accents? Living in a time-warp, Jackie, they would moan. Where's the Pretenders, Adam and the Ants, Madness?* How to answer that? *One year out of circulation is where, banged up in Durham with myself for company, difficult to accumulate shekels, you know, but give me time, eh? Give me time! You want a drink, of course I've got drink. Glasses, love? Just sup from the can, love, I promise next time I'll have some bloody glasses.*

Jackie Brown closed his eyes. *Don't think, Hovis. Don't dwell on the bitch, she ain't worth the misery.* He opened his eyes, saw the reality of life without Anna and started to sniffle, big as he was, the man began to weep. *Anna,* he moaned softly to himself. *Anna. Can't go on, Anna!*

"Mr. Dimonti", said Jackie. He'd knocked several times, opened the door but waited politely at the door-step, couldn't understand the man living in a flea-bitten hovel when he had money to move up-market. A council-house and a top-of-the-range Volvo, the car alone was worth two council houses.

"Primo, come in!" shouted a voice from within.

The interior was beautiful, immaculate. *Must have his own cleaner*, thought Jackie Brown.

"Well?" said the smaller man, his face stone.

Hovis handed over the roll of cash and began counting. Several minutes of silence as the notes were counted and stacked gypsy-fashion.

"For you, man," said Ryan Dimonti, handed over a wad of cash, delighted with the ill-gotten gains, "made my day, Primo."

"It's Hovis or Jackie, Mr. Dimonti," answered the giant carefully, keeping his head down as if he were examining the money.

He was told to sit down, maybe the height difference was hurting Dimonti's neck and the pair faced each other across the kitchen-table. The drug-dealer was smiling warmly.

"It's a term of endearment, man," said Ryan Dimonti. "*Primo Carnera* was almost as big as you, ruled the world in the early thirties."

"Ruled the world, Mr. Dimonti?"

"World Heavyweight Champion, pal." He smiled, Dimonti loved boxing to distraction, "and d'you know who beat him?"

"*Rocky Marciano*?" Jackie Brown's knowledge of the fight-game was limited, almost said *Cassius Clay* but the years seemed out of sequence. *The 1930s? Can't remember last year never mind the thirties.*

"Maxie Baer!"

"Never heard of him, Mr. Dimonti?"

"Killed a man in the ring." *Frankie Campbell, 1930.*

"With a gun?"

"A punch, pal."

"Madcap Maxie, went into movies when his boxing days were over," said an enthusiastic Dimonti. "Africa Screams, Jack and the Beanstalk." *Never the same when he was beaten by the Cinderella Man.*

"*Jack and the Beanstalk*," smiled Jackie Brown, "seen that one, Abbot and Costello?"

"Maxie Baer was the *giant* in the movie!"

Jackie recalled the movie, almost saw it all. It was Stuart Tones who had dared him to throw the firework, only a small banger. Kicked out of the cinema, barred for life. Hell of a film, always wanted to see the ending, he still remembered the fearful giant in the movie.

"Christ, no wonder Primo lost."

Ryan Dimonti smiled. *Elevator boots, bigger than Elton John's platforms!* Carnera towered over Maxie Baer, body of a giant, heart of a lamb.

"You see why I call you Primo," said the man, "you're a bloody giant!"

"Okay, Mr. Dimonti," he stood to leave but slumped back to the chair with a gesture from his boss.

"A little bird tells me," smiled the criminal, "you done some time in Durham?"

Jackie Brown nodded. It was common knowledge around the area, made front-page at the time.

"Jack Trees, The same little bird tells me you knew Jack Trees?"

"Leafy?" answered the big man. "Yeah, well, he was more of a friend with Albert Quinlan. Albert and me shared a cell, Leafy was further along, last cell. He shared with Micky Bruen. Micky had killed a cop....."

He was interrupted, "Okay, okay! Someone whispered in my ear that you done Leafy a good turn when you were banged-up?"

Hovis pulled his face. The only person he had told was Anna. Anna must have told Milly and Milly was seeing Dimonti. Milly Belling was a different kettle of fish compared to his Anna. He nodded an acknowledgement.

"You gonna tell me about it then?" He'd heard only hours earlier, Anna demanding more, playing and flirting and making her mouth go non-stop, half-listening until he heard the name of Leafy Trees. Jack Trees had been a notorious robber; post-offices, building societies and the like, rumoured he was involved in two successful high-jacks of *Securicor* armoured vehicles.

"Leafy was a close friend of Albert Quinlan, close as in sleeping together." Big shoulders were shrugged; awkward smile momentarily covered his face. "Not for me to judge, eh, Mr. Dimonti? Albert was never gonna see fresh air for years, same with Leafy, he was on a ten-year stretch. What a bitch, eh, live and let live?"

"So tell me about it?"

Albert and Leafy were already lovers when I started my porridge. It was common-knowledge on the block, just wasn't talked about. A lot of people were scared of Albert Quinlan because of what he had done to his wife. Then Micky Bruen showed his face, wanted a piece of Leafy's arse. Told Albert he would cut his throat if he interfered. Albert was getting on a bit, lost his bottle. Done me some favours, helped me read and write. Albert was a good man. He asked for a favour, I done him a favour.

"So how come you know Leafy stashed some of his dough?"

Caught Micky Bruen in the bogs, lucky really, he was taking a leak, head down staring at his piss. I knocked his skull off the tiles, smashed the tiles and he passed out, thought I'd better do a proper job on him so that he would never come back at me. Jumped on his face a few times then I left him. Heard later he was hospitalized. Never saw him again. Later, Albert and me were havin' a quiet fag in the yard and he tells me. Couple of years and Leafy would get parole. He was gonna look me up and pay me back big time, big money, like winning the pools, he said. Thought at the time it was bull-shit, made him feel better, made me feel better. Laughed when he told me, Albert, that is. Said the coppers were stupid, raided Leafy's house loads. Money was there under their noses. Albert thought it was a hoot. Leafy by name, Leafy by nature. His very words, kept repeatin' it too. You reckon somethin', Mr. Dimonti?

"I reckon something, man," said a beaming Dimonti. He looked intently at the brute. "Listen, what if I said I had some work for you that was a mite different from the heavy stuff you do now?"

"Whatever you say, Mr. Dimonti."

"Primo, you know where he's from, this Jack Trees, just curious, y`know?"

London, Mr. Dimonti. Born and bred. Didn't rate it anymore though. Said they were takin'over, the Ragheads. Lived in Southhall, near Heathrow. Nice place once, said he was sixteen when the cinema closed, opened the next week with bloody Indian films. Said he went a few times for a laugh, barred out for making a nuisance. Then it was a bus-ride to Ealing, or was it Acton? I forget sometimes Mr. Dimonti. Now I remember, he moved to Acton because he said he used to drink with Doctor Who. The first one, William Hartnell? That's the one, William Hartnell. That's how he met his wife, Mr. Dimonti. She was the barmaid, told Leafy that he was standing next to Doctor Who. Agnes. Agnes was her name. Durham lass, down the smoke workin'. Met her at the prison last year. Ma was visiting. And Agnes – that's Leafy`s wife – was chatting to Leafy. We were introduced, gave Ma something ta talk about. D'you not think prison visits are like hospital visits, Mr. Dimonti, the silence is embarrassin'. Anyway Ma and Agnes had a good old gossip. Seems Ma knew Agnes`s family. Ma had relations at Easington Lane, so did Agnes. Agnes's family lived at Elemore Colliery, about half a mile from the Lane. When Leafy got banged up in Durham, Agnes moved back North. Leafy insisted. Bought the old colliery manager's house. Big detached in a coupla acres. Leafy told Albert Quinlan that he was retirin' to Elemore Hall when he got out. That way he could keep it touch. Told Albert he liked him better than his missus.

"Elemore Hall," said Ryan Dimonti, "you know it?"

"Yeah, Easington Lane, turn left at the clock, half a mile. Colliery is closed now…the big house is on the left."

"It'll be quiet there?"

"Graveyard quiet, why's that, Mr. Dimonti?"

"Thieving?" smiled the man. "Thing is, Primo, you do this little job for me and you'll never have to worry about money again."

"You gonna rob old Leafy?" asked the thug, his mind working overtime. "You reckon his money is somewhere in Elemore Hall, Mr. Dimonti?"

"Has to be!"

"Rob from a robber," laughed Hovis, "that's good."

"You bothered?"

"Reckon Leafy owes me?"

"You want in, man, you want some payback?"

"Jesus, Mr. Dimonti," gushed the giant, "whatever you say."

"One thing," his tone went to steel, his smile suddenly ugly and "you tell no-one, understand?"

"Perfectly, Mr. Dimonti."

"You open your mouth and talk and I'll take your breath away."

CHAPTER EIGHT

Doug Mountjoy, owner of *Warren Fisheries*, was in the back-room, his chair skewed and tilted against the big peeler, his legs resting on the mound of potato sacks. Knackered was the word best describing the 30 year old. He been up since six, skinned and cut two full trays of *Norwegian* cod, peeled and chipped one large barrel and one small barrel of *Marris-Piper* chips, also, because his wife of ten years, Jenny, found it difficult to leave her bed before eleven and then had to have at least an hour before she could truly function - full English breakfast and daytime television was a priority - Doug had to prepare the patties, corned-beef, fish-cakes and cheese-patties, plus of course, the peas, curry, beans and gravy. Knackered he was, permanently.

The shop was a gold-mine in terms of the takings but the daily grind (he'd recently started a delivery service around the nearby collieries and Peterlee), made him an exhausted and occasional irritated man. After years of trying to instill some kind of discipline into his wife's head, he had reluctantly admitted defeat. It was his fault, Jenny whined, she had never wanted to work in the horrid fish-shop, it smelled so awful, not only within the premises and the preparation-room but on oneself! *Oneself,* he had whined, *taking bloody elocution lessons now*? She had been determined, more determined than he had imagined, no matter his argument or logical his replies, Jenny was adamant. She would not work in the shop. She had tried it and didn't like it, hated the shop, hated the customers!

Her apprenticeship had lasted all of eight long, stifling weeks then, in front of a queue of customers, Jenny had ripped off her apron and stormed out of the shop, walked and wept all of the way to her mother's home, stayed away a week before Doug persuaded her to return. *Thought we'd agreed to try it together, Jenny. Optilon is rumoured to be closing down. You agreed with me, take our redundancy and buy the bloody shop? What's that? It's too difficult, you can't work on a night because of the bairn? Okay. Okay. We can work around that problem; just work the dinner-time shifts, eh? Two hours, that's all.* Returned for one week then announced that she couldn't stand the smell, couldn't calculate the change for the customers, didn't care too much about the customers, any and every excuse. Doug gave up, hired a local girl: Brenda Flecker and the shop immediately improved. Brenda was a hard-working girl whose only fault was being too kind to friends and family. *Hell's Teeth, Brenda, it's not two for one, you want me bankrupt?* Six months ago Doug had taken on another girl: two afternoons and most nights. What a grafter was Joan Belling; single still and in her early twenties. *Wish I'd met you years ago, Joan. Be a bloody millionaire!* Try as he might, he couldn't get close to the young girl. *You're married, Doug, wife and bairn! You leave them and I'll think about it.* Tried every trick in the seducer's bible, it was water off a duck's back.

Doug closed his eyes, dead tired and it was only 12.30. Doug Mountjoy worked a double-shift every day, would not fully relax until ten that evening. He thought of his son, Jake, nine going on nineteen, poor beggar, dragged up, spent half of his life above a noisy shop. Fed and dressed by a frustrated, quick-tempered dad and then dumped at school before 8.30, always first in the play-ground. *Dad, why can't I go later, there's only me. Got no-one to play with.* Try explaining that to the delivery drivers when they call at the shop at nine every morning. *Collins Fish, Cracknells Potatoes, Jennings Supplies, can't be in two places at once, Jake. Sorry Jake, tell you what, son; have a word with your mother, eh? She might get out of bed for you.* What was that film he'd seen years ago. *Jack Lemmon,* definitely *Jack Lemmon*. Then he smiled as he remembered the title: *How to Murder your Wife!* There were times!

"Delivery, Doug," said Joan Belling, "Lancaster Hill, Peterlee." Doug was sound asleep, the girl shook him gently.

"Right, I'm okay!" Doug almost fell off the chair, drooling as he struggled to overcome the stupor and jumped to his feet, wiped embarrassingly at the wet mouth. "Oh, Joan, it's you."

"Fell asleep again, Doug."

Moments later and the owner was driving towards Peterlee, depression had been replaced with euphoria, glanced at the three laden carrier-bags. The order was massive. The profits would be high so Doug was on a high, switched on the radio. The *Police* were bouncing, he started singing: *Don't stand! Don't Stand! Don't stand so close to me ....*

"You want anything fryin'?" asked Brenda Flecker, "it's almost one-o-clock, better start washin' down, eh?"

Joan shook her head, "If there's any chips left I'll have a bag." She walked into the preparation-room and grabbed a wet cloth.

"Fancy a chicken," said Brenda and glanced at the younger worker. "If Doug twists his face, just say a customer ordered one then changed his mind, okay?"

Before she had time to answer a huge figure stepped into the deserted shop, "Chicken and chips, love, peas and gravy," big grin across the whiskered features as he looked at Joan.

"Hello, Hovis," said the girl, "saw you in the *Trust* with what's his name, last night?"

"Saw you," answered Jackie Brown, "in the lounge." He grinned mischievously, "Got yerself a boy-friend, eh?"

"That'll be the day, Hovis, out with mam and dad, been to *Fairworld*. Sweated a few times, didn't win," shrugged her shoulders, smiled broadly, said, "If you saw me why didn't you come and talk to me?" *Come on, Jackie, what more do I say?* "Not shy, surely?"

"Had to work for Mr. Dimonti, didn't have time."

"Not workin' today?"

"Tonight... Hudsons."

"Give me a lift home and I'll make you a cuppa?"

Stunned into a momentary silence he recovered enough to say, "Okay, Joan."

She wandered to the front part of the shop and playfully pushed him out of the shop. "You wait in the car, I'll have to mop the floor, not be a minute."

The shop-lights were extinguished and both girls began to clean the shop.

"You like him?"

"He's okay," said Joan defensively, most people knew Hovis Brown, not many had a good word for the man, only Joan.

"Big bugger, isn't he?"

"He's nice, really."

Some time later

"Ma!" shouted Joan, she turned her head and spoke to her companion, "come in Hovis, Ma won't bite you."

Jackie Brown followed through the open door. *Fifth Street*, drab and depressing from the outside, like many of the streets in the colliery but inside it was so different, warm and comfortable, fire roaring up the chimney, television blaring out its company and cheer, beautiful to Jackie, like the home he'd never had, the home he'd always wanted. While Joan busied herself with the preparation of the meal, the big man lounged against the wall between the two rooms, glancing from Joan to the television then back again.

"Switch the channel," commanded the voice.

Jackie popped his head into the living-room. Milly Belling still drugged from sleep, lay prostrate and spread-eagled across the big sofa. She was rubbing her eyes, imagined Joan had returned from work, jumped with fright at the sight of the man, started to scream but the scream died in her throat when she recognized the brute.

"Mary Mother of God!" she gasped and struggled to retain some semblance of dignity. She sat upright.

"Missus," greeted Hovis, turned to Joan, "think your mother is havin' a stroke." Jackie's wicked sense of humour.

Joan waltzed into the living-room. "Ma, which channel?" and she moved to the television.

"Tyne-Tees" and she rubbed at her face, "make a cuppa, pet, got a lousy headache." Joan disappeared into the kitchen and the older woman addressed the man. "Not workin' then?" Mrs. Belling, middle-aged, bone-idle, had never worked a single day in her life, self-opinionated too: *Men work and provide for us women. Men clock-in and clock-out. When they've finished for the day, they've finished while us girls' work round the bloody clock.* That was why Milly was eighteen stone and climbing. *I'm comin' back as a man*, she would tell anyone daft enough to listen, a politician in a frock, full of verbal diarrhoea. *Life of bloody Reilly,* she would say about men, Milly Belling, the font of all wisdom in the Belling home.

"Yeah."

"Havin' a day off then?"

"Naw," Hovis Brown knew what Joan's mother thought of him. Anna told him: *Can't stand you, Jackie, doesn't want me to see you.*

"Canny job for some, eh?"

"Almost as good as yours."

"Cheeky pup!" barked the woman and glowered at him.

He relented, told her he started work at 5-0-clock, finished when the phone stopped ringing.

"Hudsons, eh, not a proper job, is it, drivin' a taxi all night?" she huffed indignantly. "Not like workin' at the colliery, now that's a job!"

"You'd know."

"Pardon me?"

"I know, Milly, hardest job in the world," said Jackie Brown, peacemaker.

He'd had his fill, shook his head silently at Joan, winked. She grinned. Milly was given tea and chocolate and the middle-door was closed, leaving the young couple in private.

"You settled in Hartlepool, Hovis?"

The meal was drenched in salt and vinegar and red sauce. The man used his hands to pick up the half-chicken, looked fondly at the portion, said, "No choice, really, no-where else to live." He bit off an enormous chunk, chewed and sighed with pleasure.

"Still at the Headland?" Anna had told her months ago.

He nodded but did not speak for some moments while he cleared his mouth. "Bed and breakfast for a couple of weeks, then I managed to get a flat, pig-sty really, converted house with four separate rooms. Mr. Myers, the owner, calls them flatlets but they're just rooms. At least a've got some privacy."

Joan decided that only squeaking doors got oiled. *In for a penny*, she thought. "So when are you gonna show me?"

"What?"

"The flat, of course."

"You serious?"

"Of course."

"What about work?"

"Start at six."

"What would Anna say?" he mumbled nervously, "if she found out?"

Stopped in his tracks by Joan, "Shut up about Anna!"

"It's really dirty," he stammered, looked embarrassed, crestfallen. "Give me a couple of days......" He was interrupted again.

"It's only muck, I'll help you clean it, eh?" She smiled at the man and watched as he slowly acknowledged her kindness. "Jackie, let me help you?" She reached across the table and touched his huge paw of a hand, squeezed at his fingers until a slow smile touched his grizzled features. "Please, Jackie?"

CHAPTER NINE

"You okay, Joan?" Brenda was struggling with the external steel security-shutters, it was almost six-o-clock and the shop was quiet. Normally Doug kept the fan going from eleven in the morning until ten every night, noisy, but the ventilation-fan was a boon, sucking all of the smell and accumulated fumes from the two-pan electric frying-range through huge cylindrical tubing out from the shop and into the atmosphere above the shop

"Never felt better," answered the young girl. She had showered and scrubbed away the filth and stench from her body, never felt as exhausted nor as happy.

The shutters lifted, both girls trooped into the silent interior of the shop.

"Are they broken?" asked Joan.

"What's that?"

"The pans?"

"Pans are fine," said Brenda Flecker, reached under the counter, pressed a switch and the shop rumbled as the frying-range and the big fan cranked into life, the lights switched on and the pair walked into the preparation-room. "The marriage is broken."

"Again?"

"Bad this time, Doug is upstairs watching the television," she said stoically. "No windows left in the flat but he's watching television!"

"Bloody hell," she hadn't noticed the damage.

"Gotta be bad when Doug switches off the fan and won't start the shift."

"Twice this year she's left him?"

"Why the hell he married her?" Brenda placed the large plastic pail in the sink. "I'll make the batter, can you butter the buns?" She gestured towards the nearest bench, "I've microwaved the peas and the curry – they're in the Bain-

Marie - when you've buttered the last of those buns can you microwave the beans and gravy, love?"

"No problem, Brenda" and she moved away and started working.

There was a loud rapping from within the shop and a voice demanded, "You servin' or what?"

Brenda whispered to Joan, "Tell Mr. Turnbull that we've had trouble with the pans again and the shop'll open at six."

Jonty Turnbull called prompt every evening for his supper. *Fish and chips, love, not a tail-end and light on the batter.* Rain, hail, sleet, or snow, eighty years old, retired 15 years ago from the pit and as fit as a fiddle, mouth like a foghorn. *Again, be buggered.* The pensioner complained, *he wants ta get the bleedin' job sorted!* Out into the night, silently cursing and swearing, the shop-door almost taken off its hinges.

"That man!" fumed Joan as she started to butter the buns again.

Brenda carried the batter into the shop and placed it under the counter next to where she stood and fried. She reappeared, said solemnly, "I'll have another go with Doug, try and get his arse in motion."

"Has he done the chips and fish for tonight?"

"Done this mornin', that's not the problem," said Brenda. "Bloody deliveries, isn't it. We can't serve and fry and deliver. Once the bloody phone goes, Doug tends to be drivin' all night."

"See what the chat is, eh?" answered Joan. "Push comes to shove, our Anna has her licence."

"The *Nova* is goosed, Doug has said as much. Fifth gear doesn't work, keeps sayin' he's gonna change it for a *Fiesta.*"

"Doug, spend money?"

"Anna will drive for him, honest, it'll give her a night away from the house."

"She still with Corky?"

"Not for long," she smiled wistfully, "our Anna can't settle with anyone."

Nodding in acknowledgement, Brenda Flecker opened the rear-door that led to the yard. Access to the upstairs flat was through a private door in the back-yard. "I'll have a word with Doug," and she disappeared out of sight.

"Hello!" The deep throaty tones of some desperate and hungry soul echoed through the shop.

Joan moved to the front of the premises, pulled her face when she recognized the man. It was her uncle, Tyler Chandler, Ma's little brother, a sleaze-ball, thirty years old, sacked from the pit for absenteeism and vandalism: *I've spray-painted the colliery offices, have I, officer? You'll never prove it was me, there must be a dozen Tyler's in Horden! You what, so I'm the only bloody Tyler in Horden? I am? Well, maybe that makes me special, eh?* Intelligence had by-passed the fellow. *Sixpence short of a half crown,* said his own father: Joan's granddad, Tyler senior. Tyler was a skip-rat, he was also a pervert. Joan was seven years old when Tyler was the ever-so-keen baby-sitter. *Your Ma says I gotta bath you!* Joan was only a child but too old and cute for Tyler, read him like a book, the way he looked sent shivers and spasms through her. *Get away from that door, Tyler, or I'll tell my dad what you tryin' to do!* It worked. Tyler was frightened of Billy Belling, once caught him red-handed going through his sister's purse, kicked him out of the house and all the way up the street. Tyler learned his lesson and stayed away from their home for months. Joan had warned her younger sister Milly about Tyler's roving hands. *Watch him, Milly, don't believe a word he says.* Anna, thankfully was just a baby, too young for the sick deviant to molest. She told Anna when she was older about Uncle Tyler. *Never touched me, Joan, Uncle Tyler is always nice to me.* Maybe he had changed, but there was something about his eyes that scared Joan.

"Tyler?"

"Now Joan," grunted the human hyena, his smile cold and piercing as he undressed her with his eyes.

"Ten minutes, Tyler," she answered stiffly, "We're running late."

"Mind if a wait?"

"Please yerself, Tyler." She left him alone in the shop.

"Always do." He lit a cigarette and leaned on the counter. *Cold-hearted bitch*, he thought. *No wonder she's single*.

Hartlepool. Later that evening.

He drove for most of the night in a daze, in a warm and tender stupor, head in the clouds. He did not know that she had always cared about him, thinking Joan had persevered with his presence because he was seeing her younger sister. She didn't tell him straight away, it came gradually, the kindness. That first afternoon, the touching of his hand, insisting on visiting with him the hovel that was his temporary home then the drive from the colliery with carrier-bags full of cloths and cleaning materials and lotions. Not a world of condemnation as she stepped into his place and viewed for the first time the mayhem that was home.

Smiled as she wrote down the list of items to be purchased, bed-linen, duvet, pillows: crockery and cutlery and utensils, curtains and nets, a miniature vacuum-cleaner, plastic brushes, waste-bins. On and on. Joan offered money but Jackie Brown said he had enough. He left her there and went on a shopping expedition, fast as he could but didn't get back until 4.00pm, opened the door and could hardly believe his eyes. The place had been part-stripped and scrubbed.

"Take all week," she had said, "but we'll do it, Jackie."

A dozen large plastic bin-bags, chockablock with discarded sheets and curtains and festering bric-a-brac, stood like a line of roly-poly golliwogs, ready for the off. The damp and stagnant stench that binds and feeds on decaying properties had been restrained and subdued and in its place a freshness and a tang of perfume and disinfectant; a strange yet perfect combination. The rooms were brighter, the old curtains and nets pulled and bagged, the panes sparkling and virginal. The afternoon sun tantalizing as it probed and inspected for the first time, his place, almost a home. She was plagued with grime and grease, a grinning leper knowing she was overcoming the blight, smelling of sweat and mould and carbolic.

"Got to go, Jackie," could no longer call him by his silly title. "If you want, you can call on me tomorrow and we'll do it again. Do it again till it's spick-and-span?"

She scrubbed and scrubbed at her hands and blackened nails, washed them until they were blotchy and red, quickly made the bed, told him that, if he wanted, they would buy a mattress for the bed and maybe a bright *throw-over*. He drove her back to the colliery, fast and over the limit. Jackie was going to be a little late for work. He cared less. When he left her, standing like a weary angel next to his car, he could not stop himself, pulled her to him and kissed and touched her so tenderly.

"Don't know what to say," he mumbled nervously, wanted to say so much but couldn't find the words.

"Then don't say anything, Jackie," and Joan returned his kiss.

In that instant, Jackie Brown found real love, a heady cloud of mesmerizing tremors filled his body and soul and he knew that he had not really loved before. Never once known the ecstasy that comes from loving and being loved, never felt the heavenly joy that enjoined souls radiate. Jackie Brown felt reborn, he was loved! Loved!

Anna's spell had been smashed totally and forever.

Horden. 9.30pm.

"What the hell?"

"Hello, Ryan," said a smiling Anna and she handed over the parcel of food.

"What's this?"

"Hair-gel," she said, straight-faced then chuckled at her own sense of humour.

He stepped back into the room, allowing the girl to enter. "You gonna explain, Anna or what?"

Dimonti, always with his guard up, always playing the tough-guy.

She told him about Joan's desperate phone-call and Doug Mountjoy's matrimonial troubles, told him the real reason she was helping out. *Can't get you out of my mind, Ryan, can't explain how I really feel about you. One thing is certain, you drive me crazy!*

"You serious, kid?"

"Look at me, Ryan," she couldn't stop herself, first time she'd told someone how she felt about them. "It's kinda embarrassing, you think, standing here telling you how I feel."

"I see lots of women, Anna."

"Tell me something I don't know, eh?"

"And you still want to see me?" She was a beauty, probably the best of the bunch. *Look good next to him. Impress a few clients*, he thought. "You know about me, do you, Anna?"

"Talk of the place, Mister Dimonti!" placed emphasis on the *Mister*. "Never met anyone like you before."

"And you like what you see?" Blowing his own trumpet now.

"I like what I see."

"Your sister, Milly, she mentioned you were living with some punk, that not a problem for you, Anna?"

"Not a problem, Ryan." *I'll kill that witch!*

"If you want, I got people, make a phone-call," starting to believe his own distortions of the truth.

"I know you got tough-guys, Jackie Brown for one. Jackie will stand on his head for me. You know, Hovis Brown?"

"He likes you too, Anna?"

"Everybody likes me, Ryan," she said arrogantly, "but I only like you. End of story." *Please believe me?*

"You gotta understand, Anna, if I get tired of you, you gotta move on, no tantrums, no tears, eh?"

"Yeah, Ryan," she agreed, "no tantrums, no tears."

"Give me a few days, eh?" *Give me time to think straight.* "You sort things out then you phone me and we'll talk some?"

Anna beamed and kissed his cheek, touched his face then left. The shop would be screaming for her return, wasn't bothered in the slightest. She had helped them all evening, delivery after delivery. Anna checked her watch, soon be over, maybe a few more deliveries then home and a long hot bath. Cursed to herself, she wouldn't see Corky until tomorrow morning. Bloody colliery! Anna started rehearsing her farewell speech. *Corky, this is not working. I think we need some time apart? Corky. I've met a gangster. Honest to God, he told me to tell you to fuck off!* She climbed in the knackered *Nova*, laughed out loud, didn't give a hoot for Corky and grinned like the cat with the cream, all the way back to the fish-shop.

Ryan Dimonti, lights out, watched her drive away. It had happened so fast. He glanced at the free meal delivered by the girl, smiled enough to show his rather prominent front teeth. *Hair-gel!* The nerve of the woman, twenty years since anyone had dared mention his porcupine crop. He busied himself with the meal, a long time since he'd eaten so late at night, like to keep in shape. *What the hell*, he thought, thinking about the attractive seductress. *Knows how to use her tongue in more ways than one*! It might be a nice change having a bitch to look after him, three years since the last one moved out. He made his mind up, Anna could move in, at least on a temporary basis. Few years and he'd be touching forty, didn't look good a man living on his own, people might start getting the wrong idea about Ryan Dimonti.

He sat at the table, sipped at the wine, nibbled at the cod which was surprisingly succulent, drank the wine in one long draught. Starting planning and plotting, Jack Trees on his mind, remembered Jackie Brown's words: *Leafy by name, Leafy by nature,* his features crunched with confusion, what the hell did the old man mean?

CHAPTER TEN

"Hi," grunted Doug and he bravely tried to smile at the frosted face of Nora Davison, "how's Jenny?"

"Wait a minute," said the middle-aged killjoy and gently closed the door on her son-in-law.

Doug Mountjoy stood quietly, his head tilted at the heavens, felt the warm splatter of rain on his weary features, mentally counted to ten as he tried to control his growing rage. *Stafford Place*, close enough to the A19 to have permanent hearing problems: the incessant whine of traffic, the splashing rain and seemingly barred from Jenny's former home: *What could be better?* he thought.

"Doug," she said softly.

The man jumped in shock, never heard a sound of her approach, opened his eyes and saw his wife and immediately weakened. Jenny looked awful; red-eyed and puffy-faced with crying.

"What do you want?"

"You gonna let me stand in the rain, Jenny?"

"Ma's not happy at us."

"I'm not standing in the rain, Jenny," answered the man, trying to contain his irritation and anger.

"Shall we talk in the car?" The door closed momentarily as Jenny found a coat; she reappeared, sullen-faced and walked towards the *Nova.*

Doug followed his estranged wife, still counting: *One and two.....*

The engine was switched on and revved. The two mile hike to Peterlee had warmed the motor so the heater was put on full-blast. For some moments the couple sat in silence.

"Jake okay?"

"Fine."

"He at school?"

"Of course," Jenny's voice raised with annoyance, "what do you expect?"

He wanted to say so much but felt obliged to hold his tongue. There was too much at stake, mortgaged up to the hilt, fickle customers who would, at the toss of a hat, desert the shop for pastures new, a queue of delivery-drivers wanting immediate access to the premises. *Only asking, Jenny, you have a problem with getting out of bed in the morning. It's my job to drive Jake to school. Only asking!*

"Jake walk to school or did he bus?"

"Taxi, Ma sorted it out for me. I was too upset, Doug."

One and two and three.....

"Doug, are you okay?"

The man was shaking and did not know what to do or say to overcome the hurdles in front of him. He asked meekly, "What do you want to do, Jenny?"

"I'm not happy, Doug, you know that don't you?"

"What would you like to do?"

"It's the shop, the work," she started weeping. "it's not your fault, Doug, I thought I'd like it."

He tried diplomacy. "Few years we'll be able to sell up and retire, Jenny. The takings have doubled since we took it over."

"It's the work." she whispered as she struggled to find a handkerchief.

"You don't really work, Jenny," Doug said softly, diplomatically.

"That's not the point, there's no break ever. It's all day every day."

"Me not you, Jen."

"Yes and look at the state of you, it's become your life, day in, day out. Sunday and you're so tired you can't get off the settee!"

"We've got a massive mortgage..." his voiced trailed away to nothing. He was simply regurgitating the same pleas that he'd used for years, it was hopeless. He was exhausted with everything, his strength and resolve gone.

"I can't come back, Doug."

"I know." *Time to throw in the towel*, thought Doug, his heart aching in defeat. "I'll put it up for sale, Jenny, someone will buy it. I'll think of something for us."

"I'm really sorry, Doug," said the distraught woman.

Later.

The town-centre was packed but Doug Mountjoy was not wanting company. He'd left Jenny at her mother's home with the promise of action, told her he would call at the estate agents and start the ball rolling. His heart heavy, he had walked to *Bamford's* and *Dowen's* and stared morosely at the window displays. A few people past him and spoke: *Now Dougie, how's it going?* Nice people. *Hey, Doug, you made your first million yet?* Customers. Since they had purchased the business a few short years ago the man had served hundreds of folk and not only from Horden but in the nearby colliery areas and Peterlee. *Warren Fisheries* had a reputation second to none.

He trundled away, unable to initiate the demise of his dream. *Ten years*, he thought. *Ten years and I could have retired, would have been set for life. Jake would have been okay, would have forgiven me for all those early mornings dumped in the school yard, the broken promises: It's Sunday, Jake, you've gotta let me sleep. Take yourself to the recreation-ground, watch the game on your own. Ask your Ma to take you to the football-match. The lad knew the stress I was under, told him often enough. Dad, it's sunny, let's go to the beach. Ma says she won't go without you!* A few years more and he could have bought the damn beach. He walked and walked through the busy town-centre, couldn't go to any estate-agents, couldn't bear the thought of failure. He walked slowly back to the car-park and sat for an age. Jenny had left him in the past. Hell, it was becoming a regular joke at the shop. Doug thought she would stay the course, especially since she no longer worked. Too much time on her hands, too much time to dwell on the downside of it all, Jenny wasn't a bad person, happy-go-lucky once, loved him, adored the bairn but couldn't hack the new life in the shop. He thought of the home they'd sold and the happy times as a family, perhaps she was right, perhaps there was more to life than money. Doug closed his eyes.

****

The ancient Cavalier pulled up outside the terraced house. Mid-afternoon and Jackie Brown wanted to see his love, sounded the car-horn impatiently. *Toot! Toot! Toot!* Milly Belling pulled at the nets, grimaced then disappeared. A moment later and Joan hurried from the house, still wearing the shop uniform: the white tabard with the blue lettering *Warren Fisheries* across her chest.

"Jackie," smile so big it lit up her polished face.

"Fancy a ride?"

"With you, anywhere."

"Workin' tonight, Joan?" Jackie asked. He so missed her company.

"Every night and day," she chuckled, leaned across the seat and kissed his bristled features. "Doug and Jenny have fallen out big- time… she smashed the windows again."

He cared little about the domestic mayhem at the shop, crunched the gears and was away in a cloud of blue smoke.

"Anywhere nice, or is it a mystery tour?"

They spent a lovely hour wandering along the wide esplanade at Seaham Harbour, arms wrapped around each other. They sauntered about the shore-front, talking, laughing, happy and content in each other's company. A soft gentle rain soaked them to the skin: clothes drenched, hair flattened and streams running over their faces, they were in heaven.

"I'd like you to meet someone, Jack," said the girl.

"Is she nice?"

"The best!"

"Not your Mother?"

"You're getting hot."

"Your Dad?"

"You're burning."

Fifteen minutes later and the motor was chugging up the incline towards Home Hill Estate.

"Why's it called Canada?" asked Jackie, he'd driven his taxi several times to the sprawling estate. *Dumb name,* he thought.

"On the hill, highest ground in the colliery," she smiled, "always ten degrees colder up here." Joan gestured at the terraced property, "Here we are," and hurried from the car.

Alice Belling, still in the same arm-chair, roasting gently by the roaring fire, could barely stand unaided. Joan, her sweetest grandchild helped her to doddering feet. Jackie Brown stepped into the small living-room, gave a little wave and smiled openly.

"Bloody hell," said the old crone as she gazed at the giant, "it's Herman Munster!"

"Nana!" Joan feigning irritation and annoyance, smiled at the description.

"Without the bolts and screws," answered Hovis, winked at her and stuck out a huge paw, "nice to meet you."

"You're a big bugger, mind," said Alice. "Big as John Wayne, eh?"

"Bigger," said Jackie.

"And better," laughed Joan, "I'll make some tea."

77

The old woman eased her aching frame back into the bowels of the chair, told Jackie Brown to find a seat.

"Live on your own, Missus?" asked the man as he fumbled for cigarettes, leaned across and offered the packet to Alice.

"Woodbines?" asked the old girl as she squinted at the smokes. "I like Woodbines."

"Benson and Hedges any good?"

"Go on then, son," said the pensioner. "I'll try one, will you light it for me?" Then she added, "I'm Alice."

Jackie obliged and they smoked in silence for some moments.

"Live alone?"

"Husband's long gone," sighed Alice.

"Must be lonely?"

"Hardly saw the old bugger when he was alive, never missed a session at the club. Not a big drinker you understand, son, two or three pints a night." She sighed long and loud, "Still miss him."

"He work at the pit?" asked the man.

"Low-Main," said Joan as she waltzed into the room carrying the laden tray. "Told me often enough," mimicked the quaking passion of the old collier: *Joan, it's like another world down there. Hell must be better!*

Alice chucked, "The lyin' old goat, wouldn't know work if it were handed to him on a plate!"

"Nana!" rebuked the girl as she poured the tea.

"He went to the pit," chortled the woman, "but that's as far as it went." She gazed absently into the dancing flames, adding, "Twenty-two stones, couldn't tie his shoe-laces never mind do a day's graft!"

Jackie smiled, he'd found a friend.

CHAPTER ELEVEN

Thursday

Two days of threats and tears and a phone-call from Dimonti himself and Cornelius Robinson finally threw in the towel and left *Handley Street*. He'd asked his dad about Ryan Dimonti and recognized the hesitation and wavering. *Better leave, son, that Dimonti is an animal, low-life scum, Corky. Don't like him nor his family, too good to keep a decent job at the pit. Why you bothered about a girl who don't care about you, son? You gonna phone Marlon McGintey, you crazy or what, Corky. You want your head examinin'. Don't give a shit if Marlon can fight anyone, this Dimonti is in a different league, you hear me? He's into drugs and violence you wouldn't believe! You listen to your father; you pack your bags and come home, son.*

Anna told Ryan who seemed pleased, told her to be ready in an hour; they were going for a drive. The big *Volvo* pulled up exactly on time, sounded the horn as the young girl bounced out of the door. Took his breath away, looked virginal in a white skimpy outfit that showed off her exquisite shapely legs, red sneakers and a matching baseball-cap completed the picture. Anna looked gorgeous, Ryan Dimonti was right, one of the best trophies he'd collected.

"Business or pleasure, Ryan?" Anna with that cheeky voice, sat in the passenger-seat like she owned it for a lifetime, waved at her neighbour who had her nets pulled back. *Don't be jealous, Ivy.* Biggest mouth in *Horden* was Ivy Roundtree, thirty years old, eighteen stone in weight and she couldn't understand why she was living alone. "Put your eyes back in their sockets, Ivy, love," big cheesy smile for her neighbour as the car pulled away.

He told her about the proposed robbery and waited for her response. *Fantastic,* she'd said with gushing enthusiasm, *can I help. Will you please let me help you, Ryan, I'll do anything!* He carefully explained about the events that would take place Saturday. She sat enthralled and for the most part silent as the car left the sprawling housing estate. *Are you personally involved Ryan and you want me to do what?* He made a left turn and drove quickly past the bulge of factories that made up the town's industrial estate. In places the units and workshops were a stone's throw from the *Crossroads Estate,* the eastern section of *Persil Avenue,* once holding the smattering of post-war prefabs, were long gone and replaced by the *Wallpaper* factory and the sprawling headquarters of *Steadfast Security.*

He hurried on towards the small hamlet of *Little Thorpe,* eased left and took the new slip-road that fed the north route of the A19; hit the big road for only seconds before turning left again. The *Volvo* purred effortlessly in the high eighties along the wide road to *South Hetton* and *Easington Lane,* dipped into the congested high street, reached the tall obelisk that was the clock-tower then eased left and followed the signs for *Elemore.* Half a mile before the road dipped, he saw the pub on the left aptly named, *The Vale,* then lifted towards the smattering of drab terraced homes. On the right; the motley display of ex-colliery buildings followed by more terraced homes before the shrub and greenery of fields opened up. Another few hundred yards and the vehicle slowed. Both driver and passenger stared at the walled enclosure situated on the opposite side of the quiet road. Leafy Trees's home: Elemore Hall. The wide entrance, with its gates permanently open showed a gravelled drive that led to the large detached house. The car continued for several hundred yards before the winding road lifted and twisted and took the voyeurs away from their prize. Dimonti read the sign: *Hetton le Hill* and turned into a long driveway, reversed and then made his way to a vantage-point on the high-land facing *Elemore Hall*. It stood in two acres of land. The building was enormous and appeared to comprise two massive whitewashed homes blended into one monolith. It was old, probably built in the thirties or early forties. Huge mature trees and shrubs festooned the large gardens, the perimeter wall, tall enough to obstruct the view, was an irritant for Dimonti. *And for anyone else attempting to view the place,* he thought. He smiled at the realization, suited his purposes exactly and would be a barrier to any inquisitive passers-by. Drove east again towards Easington Lane, slowed when he reached the entrance of the property, looked more carefully the second time and saw the woman alone in the enormous garden, her back turned away from the entrance. Pressed his foot on the gas-pedal and disappeared from her sight, didn't want to arouse the suspicions of the female. She had to be Jack Trees's wife. Dimonti smiled coldly. She was old and scrawny, easy prey for him. Agnes Trees, Leafy's own love, decked out for gardening: wide-brimmed hat planted precariously on a wild outcrop of greying hair, overalls that disappeared into the wide-topped Wellington boots, looked the part as lady of the manor. *Not for long* he thought. *Not for long*.

"Is that it?" asked the girl.

"Is that what?"

"Are we going back home, Ryan?"

"Is that a problem?"

"It's such a nice day," she said, her eyes mocking him.

"Nice day for what?"

"Whatever you want," she teased, her hand caressing his thigh.

****

Just before three-o-clock the couple rested, warm and weary with their exertions. *See, Jackie, you can always shift muck. It's going to be so nice for us.* They sat, holding hands, as if both needed the comfort and the strength for each other. They sat sipping tea, hands clasped and talked about their future together. Talked incessantly, Jackie then Joan, like excited children in a playground, hardly taking breath, about everything relevant, anything trivial. Anything and everything, needing to unburden and share, the past, the present, their future, a lifetime of reminiscences: an endless bounty of pictures and events, shared in a fever of contentment and fond rivalry between the couple. *Cards on the table,* sighed Jackie Brown honestly.

They had made love as soon as they had entered the small flat, tender passion that erupted and wrapped them into an ecstasy of wonder, spun the lovers into a delightful fulfilling pleasure-dome, a kaleidoscope of colours bombarded them as they touched the clouds in heaven, two seemingly lost souls found again. Bliss, elation, in love and at peace with the world, the hunger for each other appeared unquenchable, unbending, they could not stop the joy and the burn and the unending delight of true love, the touching, the talking and the caressing: all vital for Jackie and Joan. So in love, so happy.

Later, as he drove her to the nearby colliery he told her about his life as a criminal, no qualms nor guilt, said it as if choices had been made that he could not negate nor cancel out, as if it were meant to be. Told her everything, from the child to the man, the petty thieving: *They weren't uncles, you understand, they were fellas havin' a good time with Ma. So I picked their pockets.* Older now and the regular raids on small corner shops. *The older kids always made me go first, can you wonder why I was always in trouble?* Progressed to car-theft, *Could never hot-wire, but I could use a hammer to knock the key-barrel, then a twist of a screwdriver. The older kids made me drive. You see, I was always the biggest. But I couldn't run fast even with a firework up my bum! Started fighting then, got out of control. Then I met Anna, she asked me to hurt those two lads. Everyone knows what happed next. Crown-court, then Durham nick.*

"I've really had enough, Joan," he said and stayed in fourth-gear most of the way home: six miles, driving single-handed, gripping and squeezing her soft fingers with his free hand. "Thing is, I don't know what else to do, Hudson's money is poor, some nights the tips are bigger than my wage! Workin' for Dimonti and I can make a hell of a lot of money and it's cash in hand."

She nodded sympathetically, happiness and love blinding and gagging her, losing all doubts and uncertainties about being on the wrong side of the law. No need to question or even rebuke. *Life can warp and distort,* she thought, nothing really mattered in life as long as she had the one who filled her heart. Her high morals were being demolished by the minute as she listened to Jackie Brown. The journey did not take long and for the most part the woman listened and plotted. *These jobs, Jackie, they can make really good money, good enough to be used as a deposit on a business? Jackie, I've always saved since I was little, haven't got a lot. Two thousand pounds in the Yorkshire. This job with Ryan Dimonti, the robbery, how much you think will be your share?*

Joan asked Jackie Brown to make a small detour around Horden. They pulled up outside the shop. *Warren Fisheries.*

"Well, Jackie," she gushed. "Say something?"

"You got me there, Joan?" The man misguidedly thought the girl was going to work early, remembered about the chaos in the Mountjoy household, heard all about

Doug Mountjoy`s personal problems. "You want me to say somethin' about what?"

"Doug wants to sell, Jackie!" She leaned across and kissed him. "If we can get a deposit, it's ours!"

"A fish-shop?" He crunched his face with apprehension.

"Makes thousands every week, Jackie," said with relish. "All you gotta do is an hour preparing and then drive the delivery-car!" Joan watched as his grizzled features lit up like a beacon.

"A fish-shop!"

"The business makes thousands, Jackie."

"Thousands?"

"As God is my witness."

"I'll call and see Dimonti tonight, Joan."

"Thought it was Saturday?"

"It is," said Jackie Brown. "Thought I'd call and see if he had any other work for me. I think we're gonna need the dough."

"Give me a kiss, Hovis Brown."

"We're a team, Joan?"

"Forever."

****

Jackie Brown followed Dimonti's direction, head west to the A19 and enter Shotton. First pub on the right: *The Gordon*. Two of the colliery's lunatics owed Ryan Dimonti a lot of money. Unknown to Jackie Brown, the Horden criminal had sent his number-one enforcer Percy Willetts the week previous to collect debts. Willetts returned to Dimonti empty-handed. *Ryan, they're like the Kray Twins, they're never apart. Either one alone I could handle, but two. In the movies it's possible, in real life, it's a no-go area.* Dimonti was going to pair Jackie Brown with Willets immediately after the robbery at *Elemore Hall*. When the

Ambling Ape asked for overtime because he needed cash, Dimonti weakened and allowed him a long leash. *Never know with these things*, thought the gangster, *might kill two birds with one stone, literally speaking.*

The *Cavalier* was on the blink again. Jackie Brown switched off the engine three times and the old motor ignored the commands and kept on rumbling. *Damn and blast*, grunted the giant and he stuck the gear into fourth gear rammed on the foot-brake and released the clutch. The Cavalier jerked then died. Manipulating the interior-light the man studied the photograph. It showed two tall and stocky smiling faces either side of a beaming Dimonti. *Friends indeed*, thought the heavy, studied the print for a few seconds then folded the photograph and replaced in his coat-pocket.

The pub appeared packed but it was an illusion. The bar was rectangular, with the counter one end and the bay-window opposite. Nearest to the window was the large billiard table which took most of the room. The long width of wall was fitted with a reddish leather bench, damaged in several places, with the occasional rip showing garish guts, it looked ready for the scrap-heap, four tables and regulation tubular chairs were planted strategically about the room. Several men were playing cards at two of the tables. A few men littered the counter, silently drinking and watching the small portable television situated up high, out of reach for the customers but accessible to the barmaid. Two youngsters tried their best to play snooker, watched by a few half-interested punters who sat or sprawled across the perimeter bench.

Jackie Brown took a mental count, thirteen men and a single barmaid. Jackie ordered a pint of lager and settled on one of the vacant stools close to the bar-counter. The big clock near to the mirror behind the barmaid showed nine-o-clock.

"Stranger?" asked the woman as she handed over the drink.

"Meeting someone," he answered, "have a drink on me, pet."

"From around these parts?" asked the woman.

The barmaid was about fifty and struggling with the pain of age, been a looker once, still had that provocative pout that once, a long time ago, would have excited most men. She was stout but refused to accept the fact, wore clothes that once clung to her figure but now screamed for space. Her hair, beautiful still, was dated, swept back off her jowls and forehead and lacquered like a magnificent mantelpiece. Black mascara and heavy make-up finished off the show.

"Horden, love."

"I always recognize a face," she said, "you ever worked as a bouncer?"

Jackie Brown smiled and shook his head, few years ago and the newspapers were full of his pretty face. *Is this face of a monster?* screamed the headlines as they showed his mug-shot next to the luckless Morrison twins: one brother blind; the other crippled. *Hartlepool shame* said another headline and all thanks to the infamous Jackie Brown.

Ten-o-clock and the two thugs made an appearance; bought their drinks and sat away from the other customers. Jackie had about an hour to decide how and when to take them out. Near closing time and a short bald man entered the pub, well-known because most acknowledged him. The scrawny stranger sat on the bench opposite the two miscreants who immediately huddled close and talked in hushed tones. Jackie Brown suddenly had an idea. He finished his drink and strolled casually towards the pool-table, both arms swing loosely by his waist. The two thugs glanced momentarily at the approaching figure then started talking again, their heads close, their attention on the bald man with them.

Jackie Brown was strolling past seemingly intent on the snooker-table, reached the table then suddenly twisted his frame so that he towered over the pair, cupped his hands around the two heads and smashed them together. The noise as skulls collided was horrendous and then he did it again. One fell forward and slumped unconscious across the table, the other thug fell slowly off his seat and fell to the carpet, his eyes rolling with pain. The bald man gasped, lifted both legs clear of the floor and assumed a foetal position.

Jackie Brown leaned close to the half-conscious thug sprawled unceremoniously on the carpet, said in a loud voice, "A warning, I've got a gun in the motor. If I come again I'll shoot the pair of you. One week to pay Mr. Dimonti!" He slapped the drooling figure with his open palm. The sound was sickening.

The dazed figure wiped away the blood from his mouth, looked up at the giant and slowly nodded.

"One week," grunted Jackie Brown, "and I'll be calling on you!"

CHAPTER TWELVE

She heard the incessant calling of the gulls as they pulled her from the deep sleep, the dawn was lifting the veil of grey from the sky and she snuggled and held him close to her damp body. Joan's eyes were focused on the chink of window that was free of the curtains, she remembered, dead of night and Jackie creeping to the big window, pulling aside the drapes and opening the pane. The night had been mild and the man had tossed and turned with the discomfort, he slept now, deep melodic breaths, his huge matted chest rising and falling in deep slumber.

The old *Cavalier* had been outside the shop the previous evening. Brenda Flecker was linking arms with Joan as they hurried from the place carrying food-parcels, laughing and smoking and pleased to leave the stifling heat of the fish-shop for the cool, fresh outside. The girls had walked past the stationary motor oblivious to the watching occupant. The loud car-horn slowed then turned them. Jackie Brown had left Hudson's Taxis on a whim. The night's takings had been pathetic, Hartlepool mid-week was always a struggle for the firm. Thursday night, normally the start of the week-end lift, was a damp-squid. Eleven-o-clock, with the reception-office oozing with impatient drivers, cigarette smoke and loud boring chatter, Jackie had had enough, called it a night and drove to Horden. He decided to drive Joan home, illogical, driving over six miles to chauffeur the girl home - home being five minutes from her place of work - but Jackie Brown was in love and a few minutes with Joan was a treasure for him.

Joan had surprised him. *Any hot water, Jackie?* When he mentioned the wall-mounted boiler that gave instant hot water when the taps were turned she had made him smile. *I'll have a bath at your place, okay, we'll share my supper, Jackie.* She had intended returning home later in the night but as she lay in the warm and cozy bed, talking and watching television, every appetite satisfied, Joan couldn't bear to leave his side. She fell asleep and only awoke when Jackie switched off the television and opened the window, his big strong arms around her again and Joan was unconscious in moments.

She stared at his stone features, eye-lids fluttering, lips gently blowing in comfortable sleep. Hovis Brown, her fella, Mister *Aggression,* all show, all blow and as gentle and as loveable as a teddy-bear. He was opening up more and more, letting his guard down and allowing her in. Two-o-clock in the morning and he was talking about his Mother, castigating and criticising her, blaming her for all of his misfortune and woe. They'd argued about it, a difference of opinion, said Joan, because he insisted his Mother had made him what he was: a failure, a loser and all his aggression and criminal ways could be blamed on his parent's. Joan had scolded, chastised and admonished him. *She's your Mother, Jackie Brown, she's brought you up on her own. Was she always so bad, can you honestly remember when you were a child?* He had tried the raised aggressive voice but Joan was a power-house of maturity and common-sense. She made him think about the early years. *Christmas was okay, I suppose. Yes, there were presents.* His features all puckered and grimaced as he recalled long-lost images. *I remember sitting in the trolley-basket going around Finefare, Mother laughing at me for grabbing sweets. Another time we were at the swimming-baths, Jesus, I forgot Ma could swim. I was always frightened of water. Ma borrowed some water-wings off another kid. She was laughing with me as I tried to paddle. You can do it, Jack. Come on, Jack, see if you can reach the side.* Lying close to her in bed, the toughest guy in the world suddenly fighting to stop the tears welling in his eyes. *There's something else, Joan, don't know if it's my imagination or you've triggered something, I was terrified of water because... because.* Jackie Brown had risen from the bed and was shaking his head. *I was in the bath and someone was telling me that anyone could learn how to swim... told me to lie on my back and I would float, said I couldn't sink.* Jackie Brown climbed out the bed and found cigarettes, lit two and returned to her side, sat moments inhaling and shaking his tousled head. *Jesus, after all these years, Joan, something like that coming back. Lying on my back, the bathtub full to the brim and sinkin', time and time again. And the man, it was a man, I remember it was a man, suddenly puts his hands on my chest and starts shouting at me, pushes me under the water and I'm drowning and calling for Ma and the man won't let go. The water is going in my mouth and up my nose and I'm hysterical.....*

An hour later, more tea and talking still, the couple wide awake, Jackie Brown in some kind of shock, the earlier recollections stinging him. He kept repeating his surprise at the recall, hidden for so long. *You never talked to your Mother, Jackie. You never asked her.* Jackie Brown had forgotten all about the incident, Joan's rebuke had been the key. Jackie on a mission now, pre-school and his home-life. *Suppose it was normal, Joan. She was clean and tidy then, a lot heavier too. Plump even.* More head shaking. *Ma's like a scarecrow now... has been for years.* Joan laughed, asking: *You gonna talk to her Jackie. You gonna stop blaming your Mother, Jackie? Good in everybody, Jackie Brown!* The man pouting like a spoilt child: *About twenty years too late, Joan. Ma and me, well we don't get along too well any more.* Joan adamant: *Give me time, Jackie Brown, give me time to work on you.*

It was ten-o-clock and Joan Belling had to get to the shop. She eased closer and kissed at the blowing half open mouth, playfully scratched at his swollen stomach. "Jackie, wake up, I've got to go to work!"

****

Albert Squires, twenty years old and in full-time employment as a milk-man was Milly Bellings newest beau. They'd been together months, ever since Albert had allowed her to drive him from the *Bell* pub to her home. He'd been drunk at the time, could hardly walk and was in no fit state to drive his new *Escort*. Milly, short, blonde like her youngest sister, Anna but without the svelte-like figure, had persuaded Albert to allow her to drive his car. Without licence or insurance, Milly, through a combination of luck and good fortune, managed to splutter her way home without incident or accident. Because he had been so nice to her Milly had allowed him to sleep on the sofa, three months later and they were still together and Milly was pregnant. Albert assumed the child was his and Milly was of the same opinion, although she had been seeing Tommy Clarke at the time and continued seeing him for about a month into her fling with Albert. She took that long to make up her mind between Albert and Tommy, both youths worked but only Albert had a car. The *Escort* clinched it for Milly.

He waited patiently outside the terraced house. He still had an hour before returning to work. Friday was a heavy shift for the youth: up at 4am with the deliveries, work until 9am; a few hours rest and then back collecting from 4pm. He tapped at the car-horn again, he had an hour before work began again. Mrs. Belling appeared at the front door, smiled or grimaced at him - Albert Squires couldn't decide - and clomped noisily down the few steps to the car. Milly stepped through the open door, gave him a little wave and an instant smile and trooped after her mother.

Albert was driving the pair to the Co-op, approximately four minutes away. *It's faster walking*, thought the youth but held his tongue, didn't want to upset Milly or her mother. Milly was out with friends that night and Albert wanted to keep her mood sweet. She was a fickle prize and he did not wish to lose her. Early hours six days a week meant Saturday night was his only evening out, a constant source of annoyance to the party-girl.

"Five minutes, Alby," said the girl as she followed the older woman towards the store.

Milly was as cute as a button and was playing on her Mother's good nature. In a short time her baby would arrive and that meant a lot of expenses. Albert's parents had promised the earth but Milly wanted the sun and the moon. Her Mother was loaded. Long-term sick benefit, plus all of her Dad's pay-packet meant Milly senior was in the same league as any professional. *Ma, Albert doesn't mind taking you for your weekly shop at the Co-op*. It sounded good enough to fool her Mother. Next door to the store was the baby-shop *Tiny-Tots* and young Milly would use her guile to persuade her Ma to window-shop. Her Mother was a sucker for the wide-eyed pout from her middle daughter.

"What do you think of our Joan, Ma?" chuckled Milly, half-heartedly glancing at the beautiful window-display of paraphernalia in the baby-shop. She slowed and looked lovingly at the gleaming pram. *My pram*, thought Milly.

"Beats me what she sees in that lump," answered the woman and she joined her daughter at the window.

"Only a few weeks ago and Hovis Brown was asking about Anna."

"He was keen on her," agreed the mother.

"Went to jail for her!"

"Those poor Morrison boys, lives ruined," she muttered, stared at the display. "Nice pram, Milly." She pondered a moment before adding stoically, "Apparently they're copin' well enough on disability benefits."

"Should have kept their gobs shut about Anna," offered Milly. "You wouldn't believe what they said about her."

"She told me."

"Made Hovis lose his temper, good and proper."

"She always goes for the Crackerjacks," said Milly, "Our Anna."

"Crackerjacks?"

"Hovis Brown and now Ryan Dimonti."

The mother turned slowly and faced her daughter. "Anna is seeing Ryan Dimonti. No one told me."

"It's a fact, think she's been sleeping at his house all week."

"Don't like the Dimontis at all, especially the dad."

"What's wrong with Ryan's dad?"

"I went to school with his mother, Nichola. What a twisty bitch she was, always bringin' notes so that she could miss lessons. In a wheelchair now, never been happier, can moan in peace all day long. Bloody arthritis, that's all she's got. I've had it for years, never hear me complain."

"I've never heard you complain," agreed the girl. *Look at the pram, Mother, it's a bargain!* "You've always managed your housework, Ma."

"Ryan's dad?" prompted the girl.

"John Dimonti, liked me for years," said the woman proudly.

"You got the looks, Ma." *The pram, Ma, look at the pram!*

"Wasn't normal," continued Milly senior, "not like other men, you know?"

"In what way, Ma?"

"You know, pet," smiled and pulled her face. "You know the way men are...."

"Led by their dicks."

"Wasn't interested in messin' about," chuckled the woman, adding quickly, "not that I did anythin' like that, you understand. He didn't even try which I found very strange."

"Right," said the girl, "shall we go in the Co-op, Ma?" A final glance at the display, "Look at that pram, Ma, it's so expensive, isn't it?"

Milly senior shook her head knowledgably, "That's a bargain, Milly. If we had time," and she glanced at the vehicle parked close, observed the miserable face of Albert Squires, "we could have a look inside."

"Albert won't mind, Ma," said a relieved Milly and she led her Mother into the shop.

"Anna was tellin' me, Ma," confided Milly, "Hovis works for Ryan Dimonti."

"Wouldn't surprise me in the slightest, pet," pouted the woman, "they're all tarred with the same brush. Now let's have a look at that pram."

CHAPTER THIRTEEN

Saturday evening and Jackie Brown parked his old motor in Kent Walk, Horden, a few minutes walk from Ryan Dimonti's home, didn't want any connections linking him to the drug-dealer in the event of any screw-up with the job. No way was he going to be snared and caught like a dog if something bad happened. He wore the old overcoat, liked it so much, not only the colour, black, but the deep pockets inside the garment. Hide a house if you wanted, tonight he had a hammer hidden. With a bit of luck he might be leaving all this life behind, all he needed was some hard-earned luck. He was owed, had saved Leafy Trees's bacon when he was banged-up, promised a fortune after he had taken good care of Micky Bruen. *People call me Mad Micky, you hear me*? Some tough guy he was, lying on the lavatory-floor, pissed his pants, he was that tough! Jackie had stopped the lunatic in his tracks and allowed the two old goats to have quality-time alone. He was definitely owed. He reached the council-house, still couldn't work Dimonti out, a *Volvo* sitting in the street just waiting to be damaged by some young punk with nothing better to do, not even garaged. Where was the sense in that? He hurried down the foot-path and knocked at the door.

"Anna?" said an amazed Jackie Brown.

"Hello, Jackie, you want to come in, Ryan won't be long."

He stood rooted to the step, head shaking slowly as if he didn't understand.

"Why you shaking your stupid head, Jackie," asked the young girl, "you not feeling too well?"

"Why you here, Anna?" He mumbled, "Mr. Dimonti and…."

She stopped him with an upraised palm, "Cut the crap, Jackie!"

"Anna, you and me," Jackie Brown took a deep breath, did not wish to hurt her despite all she had done to him but he was stronger now. He was with Joan. He loved Joan. Anna, no matter how she begged, was in the past. "It's over!"

Big smile answered him, "Idiot!"

"You what?"

"Bloody idiot to think I want you!"

"You don't?"

It was the female's turn to shake her head. "I live here, Jackie, you got that?"

"With Mr. Dimonti?"

"Who else lives here, idiot?"

The insult rattled him enough for Jackie to reply with sarcasm, "He's seeing Milly. I picked her up the other mornin' about two-o-clock. You both live here, you both sharin' him, Anna?"

"Piss off!"

Full of bravado he surprised himself when he snapped, "Dimonti in the middle, you and Milly either side, eh?" He grinned at her, enjoying his new-found freedom, the shackles between then broken forever.

He heard movement, the garden gate behind him crashing noisily. Ryan Dimonti strode purposely along the path, carrying a hold-all, acknowledged the bigger man and entered the kitchen, gestured for Jackie to follow.

"You two know each other, yes?" A little glance at both of them before he turned to the man, "Anna is a part of this now, okay?"

"Thought we was robbin' the place?"

"We are!"

"We don't need Anna."

"Who the fuck you talking to, moron!" Dimonti incensed at the attitude of the hoodlum.

96

Jackie Brown lifted his hands in a gesture of uncertainty, looked at one then the other, saw the smirk radiating from the girl's face.

"I asked you a question, moron?"

He backed down graciously, head bowed he whispered, "Sorry, Mr. Dimonti."

The silence was deafening, three people close together and no one speaking, everyone thinking.

Dimonti spoke first, told Jackie and Anna to find a seat. They sat at opposite sides of the small kitchen-table, Jackie still had his head lowered. Anna watched Dimonti's every move.

"Change of plan," he directed his words at the big man. "The house won't be empty, Leafy's wife will be there. I've had someone watch the house all week. She never leaves the place." The man could lie so easily, made him sound professional and calculating. "That's why Anna has been brought in." He stepped up to the seated figure, prodded him with a finger, "You still listening, Jackie Brown?"

First time he had called him by his proper name, caught his attention immediately, glanced up and nodded uneasily.

"Anna will knock on the door, when Leafy's missus answers the door, Anna will frighten her by showing her this." Dimonti walked to the draining-board on the sink, grasped at the zipper on the hold-all and opened it, grasped the implement and threw it on to the kitchen-table. The big knife clattered noisily over the wooden surface. Jackie and Anna jumped with shock. "Anna then goes in the house, then I'll follow, easy?"

"Not too sure, Mr. Dimonti," answered Jackie sullenly. "She's seen me at the prison more than once, talked to me and she'll remember your face ...pick you out of a line-up!"

"She'll pick me out of a line-up, eh. An identity parade you mean, you saying I stand out some?"

"It's the spiky hair, Mr. Dimonti," said in a whisper, kept his head down. *Look like Wurzil Gummidge*, he thought, waited for the blows.

"Hey, Jackie," said Ryan Dimonti, "what do you reckon?"

Jackie Brown looked up, gasped in shock. The man wore a shiny black hood which totally covered his head, two large grotesque holes had been cut for eye-holes.

"You see my hair," he mocked, "you see my spiky hair now?"

Jackie shook his head.

"Anna, show him!"

Anna stooped and pulled at the contents of a plastic carrier-bag. The long auburn wig totally altered her appearance. When she fitted the horn-rimmed spectacles she looked so different. Jackie Brown couldn't believe the change.

"You okay now?" asked the boss.

"Okay for you two," said the huge fellow, "thing is with me…"

"I understand your worries, Jackie, there's not many giants about. You do stand out a little. I take your point. A hood will help but I can't cut off your legs, eh?" Dimonti cracking jokes and thinking he was a comedian.

"Somethin' like that Mr. Dimonti."

"So what if I tell you your job is to wait outside in the car. If Leafy's missus has company that we can't handle then I'll use you as back-up. Okay with that?"

"Okay, Mr. Dimonti."

"It's almost ten, what say we have a drink to celebrate, eh?"

Minutes later and the three walked away from the council-house. The two men were carrying their disguises; the woman wore hers and looked the part. They reached the car; the *Escort* had seen better days, pride of the scrap-yard.

"You drive, pal," said Dimonti and he threw the key at Jackie Brown. "Anna, you find a place in the back, it's a bit messy, got it for free so don't grumble." He watched her struggle over cardboard boxes and festering magazines. "When we get back, I'll put a match to it."

Twenty minutes later and they had reached Elemore Hall.

A moment before turning into the gravelled driveway, Jackie Brown switched off the car-lights. The vehicle bumped and scrunched across the sea of grit, stopping close to the large rear-door. Both men pulled on their disguises, the driver stayed in the vehicle while Dimonti and the girl climbed out. Opposite the door-way was a large bricked building, a double-garage and from within a dog started howling. The couple ignored the agitated barks and yelps and moved towards the door. Dimonti positioned himself at one side, hidden by shadows and untidy shrubbery. Anna, the weapon hidden behind her back, banged loudly on the door.

Lights clicked on to the left and a night-light suddenly blazed above the door-well, bolts and locks were clattered and cranked and the door eased open by inches.

"I'm sorry to bother you, love," pleaded a desperately-sounding Anna, as if she were born for the part. "My car's broken down, I'm on my own, could I call home please?"

The ploy worked. The door was closed momentarily while the security-chain was lifted.

"Come in, pet," she said, glimpsed the long silver blade of the knife and started to swoon and gasp for air.

Anna pushed her hard and the woman careered heavily back into the hallway, all the while gulping and retching and clutching at her throat. Her eyes bulged as she watched a second figure loom into the doorway, wearing a black hood. Her body went into involuntary spasms, pain erupted through her chest and into her screaming skull, pain like she'd never felt before. She knew she was dying, never thought of Leafy, or her still-born son, Nathen, all those years before. The last thoughts that racked through Agnes Trees's demented head wasn't even the fact that she'd forgotten to take her angina-pills again - *waste of time doctor they're only bloody asprins* – but the idea that she hadn't changed her underwear. She'd worked in the garden all day and was about to shower and change: *What'll they think when they find me, sweet Jesus, they'll think me dirty*! Her head seemed to burst into bright lights for a second, images of soiled and sweaty underwear and excruciating pain all shrieking at her, bombarding her mind as she fought for breath, probes of whiteness and pain ricocheting through her body like electricity. Suddenly, thankfully, everything went black for Agnes Trees.

The intruders stood transfixed for some moments, unsure as to what they were witnessing. In the background, a television blared and shared a nightmarish stage with the yapping whining dog. The couple stood and stared as Agnes Trees died. Jackie Brown loomed in the doorway, minus hood. He knew something would go wrong, felt it in his guts. Dimonti, sensing his presence, turned and looked at the big man filling the doorway and removed his hood.

"Hell of a start!" he gasped, his features were white and perspiring, didn't look like a tough guy anymore.

Jackie sensed this; eyes left Dimonti and fell on the wooden effigy that was Anna. *Bloody hell*, he thought, *they've both bottled! It's up to me, it's up to me!* He'd been through enough shit to last a lifetime, Jackie Brown was resolute, knew he had to finish the job. He closed the door, saw the switch that operated the night-light and clicked it off. Moments later and the mutt stopped its mad barking.

"Mr. Dimonti," he said strongly, "we gotta finish the job." He pushed gently at his boss. "Want your gloves on now, Mr. Dimonti, you hear me?" shoved him a second time and watched as the man came out of the stupor, "Gloves, Mr. Dimonti."

100

Ryan Dimonti fumbled with the gloves and watched as Jackie Brown knelt next to the crumpled figure, saw the big man touch and caress the skewed, wrinkled neck, bit his lip as his henchman confirmed his fears.

"Dead as a Dodo," said Jackie Brown. He moved to Anna who seemed oblivious to it all, like an abandoned mannequin with arms over her chest, the large blade of the knife protruding above her slim shoulders. "Anna, we gotta do this," shook her awake, watched her tearfully nod.

"Mr. Dimonti," Jackie Brown taking control, "coupla days they'll find her, think she's had a heart-attack. They'll never know we've been here, all we gotta do is take our time and keep the place neat. Mr. Dimonti!"

The man began to regain his composure, said, hesitantly, "Okay, okay, I know what we have to do." He moved away from the hallway, saw the wide girth of the spiral staircase and started gingerly climbing.

"Anna," said Jackie, "put on your gloves and check every drawer in the main room, okay?"

She walked slowly towards the sounds of the television. He followed her and took away the big knife, put it in his deep coat-pockets.

They left at one-o-clock in the morning. The total cache amounted to a bagful of very expensive jewellery, four *hall-marked* silver goblets; a signed photograph of *Laurel and Hardy;* a blue-speckled vase, two feet tall with no discernable distinguishing marks anywhere on its base: *It's a bloody blue smudge, Anna*, warned an invigorated and revived Ryan Dimonti: *Fit for a car-boot sale*. And cash. Lots of cash, fifteen bundles, each totaling one thousand pounds found by Jackie Brown in the false base of the large dressing-room table. Jackie was given four wads; Anna received one, Dimonti kept the rest.

They spent the last half an hour tidying up and covering their tracks. *Clean as a whistle*, said Anna, perky now that the worst was over, checked and double-checked.

The house was left as they had found it, apart from the stolen items. Neat and tidy, apart from the crumpled and heartbreaking remains of Agnes Trees, whose eyes staring blankly at the door, mouth wide and dentures hanging loose from her gums in a manic smile. They stepped over her and around her and made their way out of the home, closed the door but left it unlocked. The dog did not start its frenzied barking until the car revved and jerked its way out of the grounds.

The drive back to Horden was endured with a pensive silence. Jackie Brown did not want to converse with the others, his head was racing. He had other plans which was why he did not complain at his meagre share of the ill-gotten gains. He desperately needed to borrow the car. He pulled up near to McGuiness Avenue.

"You want, Mr. Dimonti, I'll fire the car?" waited for the rebuke or abuse but none came.

An exhausted Dimonti nodded gratefully, said wearily, "You'll do that for me, Jackie Brown?"

"Anything, Mr. Dimonti," answered the giant, "grateful for the money."

"Okay, you do that tonight and I'll see you tomorrow. Worth £50, okay?"

"Do it for free, Mr. Dimonti." He watched them both trudge away into the night, Dimonti carrying the two small bags, Anna struggling gamely with the unwieldy vase. *Professional thieves or pantomime thieves*, thought Jackie, checked his wrist-watch, smiled a giant's smile, he'd take a slow ride back to Elemore Hall. The death of the woman had shocked Dimonti enough for him to forget the big picture. The money they had found wasn't the jackpot, far from it. He recalled Leafy's words: *Leafy by name and Leafy by nature*. Jackie had thought a lot about it, had to be something to do with leaves, common-sense, knew it for a fact. Couldn't understand the two accomplices not comprehending, two so-called bright-sparks. *Self-praise*, he thought, *maybe Jackie Brown wasn't so stupid after all?*

He threw caution to the wind as he reached the big house. Car-lights extinguished, only the scrape and splatter as the gravel shrieked his arrival, through the open gate and he skewed right and headed away from the residence. A splattering of bright stars became heavenly candles as he bumped and pushed over small mounds and ornate paths and occasional flower-beds before resting under a huge overhanging tree. Jackie Brown waited a while and allowed his eyes to acclimatise then he was out and clambering on to the roof of the motor, stretching and heaving his huge body up on to the branches like some retired Tarzan. Wheezing like some middle-aged consumptive as he clung perilously to the shivering branches. *Just call me*, he gasped, *Jungle Jim*. He stood quaking like a human gorilla, mouth sucking in the cold night air, head looking this way and that, didn't know what he was looking for, only knew he would recognize it when he saw it. *Jackie Brown's logic.*

That's the one, he said to himself. He'd struggled slowly up to the highest branches inch by inch. Minutes before he'd touched something warm and he'd screamed, the owl shrieked and he'd only managed to keep his balance. His hand, still trembling, had touched the artificial object, a box-like shape, fingers prizing and playing with the shape: the bird-house, a wooden bird-box without an opening! *There you go Leafy. Leafy Trees's own safety-deposit box*. Jackie grinned like a hyena. *Maybe one per tree?* He wrapped an arm around the trunk and with the big knife in the other, began to twist the blade into the screws that held the contraption. It took five minutes of back-breaking work. Loose now and Jackie pulled the box free from the trunk and carefully threw it to the earth. *One down*, he muttered. *How many to go?*

The dawn was breaking over leaden, reddened skies as he bumped his way from the gardens and on to the gravel. The dog had given up its protestations and stayed asleep, out through the gate Jackie manoeuvered the rust-bucket of a car. He would drive to Hartlepool and leave the vehicle with its door open and the key intact, next to the shops. Perhaps park it outside *Norma's Tea Shop*. There was always people hanging about the Headland's only café. It might not be stolen for at least an hour. He smiled at the thought and glanced at the passenger-seat. Three boxes and not a birds-nest in sight. Three boxes with an amateurish attempt using ink-marker to draw a circular black hole on their fascias. From the garden looking up to the trees who would guess that the circles weren't entry-holes for the birds? Leafy must have told Agnes what to do. *You can do it, old girl. Pretend you're Rolf Harris. Just a dot, then circle around the bloody dot with an ink-marker. Climb the trees, of course you don't climb the trees, use a bloody ladder, woman!*

Hit the jackpot, Jackie Brown? Three boxes each containing ten plastic-wrapped wads of cash, £30,000 in total, add that to the earlier present from Dimonti and the man was rich. He thought of Joan, the way she cared about him, telling him they were going to make it. Jackie and Joan, what a team!

My name? My name is Jackie Brown, I own the biggest fast-food shop in Horden! That Mercedes, it's mine of course!

Jackie Brown's dreams had all come true.

CHAPTER FOURTEEN

Agnes Trees lay three days alone in the big house, Leafy's fault as usual. They had fallen out the previous Friday, Leafy's intransigence was the reason Agnes had walked out of the visitor's room at the prison. At least two years left of his sentence before any chance of parole and Agnes was annoyed at his inflexibility. *Half a bloody mile,* he'd muttered angrily, as far as he was concerned she could take a slow stroll to her sister's house in the Lane. *It's more like a mile,* she'd protested, *I should know I've walked it, in the bloody rain and snow.* A few years earlier he'd relented and agreed that Agnes could return to the North-East. It suited him; too many so-called friends were calling on Agnes and she was only human, after all. There were other, probably more important considerations to think about. Their flat in Acton, West London, was too small to keep all of his loot. Agnes, even though he'd purchased a loft-ladder, was having trouble climbing into the loft, always bloody complaining was Agnes. When Elemore Hall had come on to the market, Agnes was ecstatic. Her words: *I'll be able to walk to our Rachael's house.* Rachael was her younger sister and lived a mile away in Easington Lane.

The honeymoon between the imprisoned crook and his estranged and emotional wife didn't last, months in and she was whining like a lost cat. *Too isolated, Leafy, I'm frightened on my own. Nobody calls. There's only our Rachael but it's too far to walk and the buses are non-existent! Learn to drive, Leafy? I'm too old!* Moan, moan, moan! *You've gotta stay, love. All the cash is hidden there. It's a bloody mansion, you ungrateful bugger, your stupid sister lives in a dirty council estate! You don't care, that's where you want to live? Then go, take a hike!* And she had, grabbed her coat and bag and stormed out of the crowded visitor's room. Embarrassed Leafy no end. That was Friday.

It was Albert Quinlan who had persuaded Leafy to make the phone-call. Albert cared enough about his lover to rise above his own selfish needs and desires, knew the real reason why Elemore Hall had been bought, been told often enough. *I'll be able to visit you, Alby. Don't you want me to visit?* Of course he did, loved the gangster beyond distraction and could listen all night to his tales and fabrications. He'd heard them all until he was word perfect, still made him laugh, what a delightful rogue was Leafy Trees. But Albert also knew life, knew enough to know that when Leafy got his freedom he'd be gone. Not immediately, could be weeks or even months but their companionship, their bond, would be invariably severed once the reality cut its mark on Leafy Trees.

Leafy had swallowed his foolish pride and phoned his wife, Agnes. Tuesday had been a long and frustrating day for the jailbird. *At her bloody sisters, no doubt, what the hell do they talk about all day?* He'd moaned to Albert Quinlan. The evening came and still there was no response from his spouse. *Doing it on purpose, Alby, wants me to sweat!* Finally, Leafy, chided by Albert Quinlan, reluctantly confided in Gordon Briggs, one of the more decent screws, about his anxieties. 11.30 that night, Leafy Trees heard the awful news. His beloved wife had died from a heart attack.

Leafy Trees, no longer a threat to society, was allowed out to attend the funeral. Rachael, Agnes's sister, was a trooper, sterling in her efforts to make the day one to remember. Supervised everything, arrangements were taken care of in a professional and polished manner, impressed Leafy enough to ask her and her dumpy, harassed, husband, Raymond, to live rent-free at Elemore Hall. Unsure initially, Leafy soon persuaded them, like the Pied-Piper he was, his tongue the teasing pipe: *You've bought your council-house, Rachael, that's fantastic news.*

Rent it out, rent it out and live like a lady at Elemore Hall. Try it for a few years? Jack Trees needed someone living in the big house, not only for security against the elements but as a safeguard against would-be burglars and thieves. If only Leafy had been able to visit his property and see inside his palatial home, he would have known immediately that burglars had already visited. The jewellery; the vase; the silver-ware; all worth a small fortune were all missing. If he'd walked the garden he would have suffered the same fate as his late wife, the missing bird-boxes would have triggered a heart attack. The blame lay with Agnes. She had let it be known to her only sister that she wanted her last hours on earth to be at her mother's old home - Rachael had bought it when their mother had died. *Rachael. If I die first I want to be brought straight to this house, you hear me, Rachael. You bring me to Ma's house or as God is my witness, I'll haunt you and Raymond!* Agnes Trees didn't want to be left in a coffin in the big and bleak *Elemore Hall*. The quirk of fate played perfectly into the inept burglar's hands. The theft would not be discovered for another two years.

On the same afternoon as the funeral, two rather excited people were escorted into the upstairs flat belonging to Doug Mountjoy. The bedroom windows had been replaced and the side-window in the living-room, although sealed with heavy cardboard, was due for repair within days. The owner was still deeply depressed with the sad turn of events. The knowledge that Jenny was not returning to the family home had saddened and shook him. It was the two employees, Brenda and Joan, who had insisted on opening the shop every day. The takings had dipped by a third, mainly due to the lack of a delivery-driver. Anna, Joan's sister, was erratic and irregular, starting late and finishing whenever the mood took her. No matter how they had tried, Doug Mountjoy could not fight the depression that overwhelmed him and would not leave the flat and commence home-deliveries.

"And you have the capital to sweeten the mortgage people?" asked a disillusioned and damaged Doug.

"Between us," Joan nudged her partner, "we've over half already. The Yorkshire Building Society liked the look of your books, Doug and the family have chipped in and loaned us enough."

Joan, taking on the role of chief cashier, had persuaded all of her family, apart from Anna, to accept cash from her and to take it to the *Yorkshire Bank*. She had prudently given them their account number: even prepared paying-in slips in case of mishap or error. Her family, she had reliably informed Jackie Brown, had the intelligence of newts. *Not Newton, Jackie, love, newts!* The Yorkshire Bank had been impressed. *The couple was only borrowing £10,000 over twenty-five years*, said an enthusiastic Andrew Colledge. *The business accounts provided by Mr. Mountjoy were excellent and a joy to read. The shop was an astute profitable business with much potential.* They were mindful to accept the young couple as soon as it was appropriate.

"Right then?" said a morose and sickly Doug, almost out of his mind with a mixture of grief and relief; everything appeared to be happening too quickly for his liking.

He had not even advertised the shop so confused and uncertain was he. Goaded by a revitalized Jenny, barracked by his mother-in-law, it was as if the sale was taking on a life of its own. Approached by Joan Belling, normally so quiet and demure: *Could I borrow your business books, Doug, the bank won't even consider a loan unless you produce the books.* Everything happening at breakneck speed: Jenny seeing a solicitor and starting the process; oiling the cogs: *Sweet Jesus, a solicitor, Jenny, can't we talk about this? Is there any need to be so hasty, shouldn't we talk more?* It was as if he had no control over his destiny. His dreams of riches and success were but a damp squid now. Still desperate that events might alter again, he hesitated and vacillated when faced with the young couple.

"Shall we have a few more days to think about it then?" offered doubting Doug. *Who knows what tomorrow might bring?*

"No," answered a resolute and annoyed Joan, folding her arms showing her mood, "you said if we could get a mortgage then the shop was ours!"

He moved to the only window-pane that wasn't broken, stared blankly at the street below. "You're only a child, Joan, it's going to be a lot of worry on your shoulders." He persevered with the ploy, "Self-employment is hellish, love, the constant work, the accumulated stress. You can't clock-off and simply go home… it's seven days a week, every bloody week. Look at me, Joan, it can break a marriage!"

Jackie Brown, who had appeared to be part of the closing chorus-line, stepped to the window and looked down at Doug Mountjoy, fiddled with something that appeared to be lodged deep within his trouser-pockets. He said hopefully, "Mr. Mountjoy," pulled out a plastic covered roll of twenties, "suppose I give you this as a present, for your back-pocket?"

Doug dragged his eyes away from the drab streets below, saw the money and his eyes lifted to the giant. "How much?"

"£1000."

"Make it £2000."

"£1500, I'll shake your hand on the deal?"

Doug Mountjoy knew the worth the business; he also observed the keenness and determination from the prospective buyers. A determined Doug pushed his luck, played his bluff, looked at the big man and then at the anxious girl. "I really don't want to sell, Joan, it makes so much money."

"£1750 and that's my final offer," said Jackie Brown.

"£2000," he was resolute, glanced again at the girl and played with the psychological muck, "and I won't mind if you walk away." *Never show too much interest,* thought Doug Mountjoy.

Jackie Brown glanced at the woman, saw the mix of heartache and hope radiating from her face, her mouth pinched in anticipation, could read her mind like she could read his. *For us, love,* he thought. *Me and you.*

"£2000 it is," said the big man and he stuck out his hand.

The two men shook hands. Jackie Brown and Joan Belling would soon be the proud owners of *Warren Fisheries.* They walked down the stairs and out of the shop, ignored the car, wanted to walk and talk. Joan floating on air. It appeared unreal and yet so real, she started singing spontaneously, so unlike her to show any emotions, grasped at the man's arm, her voice loud and clear.

You shall have a fishy, on the little dishy... Sing with me Jackie... *You shall have a fishy, on the little dishy... ...*

Jackie, turning scarlet, joined her: *When the boat comes in.*

The couple stood in the middle of the back-street, arms wrapped around each other and they kissed passionately. They didn't notice the man at the window of the flat, did not see his tears falling. Doug Mountjoy turned away sobbing, his heart was breaking, his hands covering his anguished features.

CHAPTER FIFTEEN

"Hello, miss," said the stranger, six feet-two, 240 pounds of solid muscle, mid-thirties, head shaved ominously which highlighted the cobweb of weal's and scars that seemed to cover the full pate and neck of the man like some perverted fleshy road-map. Micky Bruen was dressed casually, thin, zip-up jerkin and baggy jeans, the trousers were turned up several inches showing the brown work-boots.

Alice Crabtree, twenty-two, pencil-thin and frumpy gasped at the man, made her all hot and bothered. *He's gonna grab me and take me away. Maybe throw me into his bed-sit and tie me up tight.....*

"Miss?"

She recovered enough to gasp, "No vacancies, pet."

"Excuse me?" *I look like I want work, missy?*

"You are after a job, aren't you, Mister......"

"This is Hudson's," said the man, pulled out the cigarettes and searched for a match, "smoke?" handed the packet to her. She shook her head; the man shrugged his shoulders and replaced the packet, found the lighter and lit the cigarette.

"Yes, this is Hudson's," said Alice Crabtree proudly, "biggest taxi-firm in Hartlepool." She had worked for the firm since she had left Dyke-House School more than four years before. Five good passes at *G.C.S.E.* and a *Computer Awareness Certificate.* Alice, in her own mind at least, was a star. "I am the chief controller."

"Important position," he answered softly, "I bet you're very proud, eh?"

Alice wasn't sure if the stranger was making fun of her and said, ever so carefully, "You taking the piss, Mister?"

There was a little stammer in her voice, a weak smile that resembled a grimace. Alice Crabtree was a gentle soul at heart, hated confrontation. Any irate customers were immediately put on hold and then ignored, bit of an ostrich was Alice. Luckily there had been very little trouble at the taxi-rank. She had always called for backup from the fleet of drivers, twenty-six at the last count, especially drivers like big Hovis Brown. It had been a shame he'd put his notice in to Mr. Hudson.

"Certainly not, love" and the stranger smiled.

Alice thought he was ugly nice, looked ferocious and yet there was something gentle about him, she asked, "Okay, how can I help you?"

"I'm trying to find my cousin?"

"Shouldn't you try the police or the council?"

Got it in one, little girl, just been to the council, told them some hard-luck story about Jackie Brown, needed to get in touch with him urgently! No luck with the Council, shoulda slapped the jerkoff with the suit. But, hey, gotta keep cool, like it's nothing important, not when you got all the time in the world. Thank you, Mr. Clerk, you have a nice day. Go to the police, I don't think so. I'd be shackled and deported back to the Smoke, just a few outstanding warrants for me. Thanks but no thanks. Then I got my head together, didn't I? How many people coulda worked in a circus? The man was almost seven feet tall, Jesus! Struck lucky in some flea-pit of a pub next to the train-station. Everybody knew the man, Jackie Brown this, Jackie Brown that, only just missed his whore of a mother by minutes! Some mother, punters wanted to talk about her not her dolt of a son. Got his address. It was some dilapidated doss-house on the so-called Headland. William Myers, the owner of the slum had said that he'd suddenly given his notice, then the taxi-firm was mentioned. That's why I'm here with you, sweetheart.

"Yes, love, they sent me to you." He explained why he needed to find Jackie Brown.

"Should be working his notice this week," offered the receptionist/controller, "hasn't shown his face though. If he does call, do you want to leave your name and I'll pass on a message?"

"Micky Bruen, tell him Micky Bruen is looking for him." He ambled towards the open door.

"Hey, Mister," said the girl, "I've just thought of something." A big goofy grin covered her face.

With those fangs you can tell me anything, missy. "Okay, I'm all ears" and he smiled at the receptionist and stared at her teeth. *Just needs glasses and she's Janet Street-Porter!*

"Jackie's getting married."

"You don't say?" He had a second thought. *Maybe Ken Dodds's daughter?*

"Yeah, told me himself."

"He tell you where?"

"No but he's buying a fish-shop!"

"You don't say." *This gets better and better,* thought Micky Bruen.

"Horden."

"Is that the name of the shop, miss?"

Her face twisted with annoyance: *Taking the piss, definitely taking the piss.* "It's a place Mister!"

"You tell me where, miss?"

"Horden Colliery, Mister," she replied frostily. "Few miles up the coast."

"You be a bit more specific, miss?"

"Buy a map, eh?"

"Have a nice day, miss," he muttered belligerently. "Oh, by the way, miss, I can recommend a good dentist. A hell of a dentist, shoulda seen what he done with Freddie Mercury!"

The young receptionist gawked and watched the thug disappear. Seconds later and safe from retribution she found the strength to retaliate, "Bastard, have you looked in the mirror lately?" She was shaking with anger. Alice Crabtree was so incensed at the man's outburst she left her desk and walked to the small cubicle that led to the single lavatory. She stood for several minutes gazing and posing in front of the small mirror, even smiled at herself. *My teeth,* she pouted petulantly, *are beautiful,* then she realised why the stranger had acted so rudely. *Forbidden fruits,* thought Alice with a smug look on her face, *he wanted her but couldn't have her!*

Micky Bruen walked along the street and found the car, bit of a struggle getting into an Austin Mini. *Still beggers can't be choosers, he thought,* not like he paid for it. A day ago it was parked up in *Gunnesbury Lane* in *Acton,* opposite the *White Swan.* Sheer luck for Micky Bruen, left the pub and saw the young black kid stroll from the mini and parade along the garage-front, eyeing up the motors. Micky watching as some gargoyle from the Caribbean, struggling to walk with a ton of gold draped around his bull-neck, grabs the kid as if he were some long lost relative. *Car-dealers,* thought Micky, *biggest thieves on the block.* The salesman, holding on to the youngster like he was some precious thing, waltzes him into the showrooms, out of sight. *Hey,* thinks Micky, *my fault some jerk leaves keys in his motor*?

Michael Bruen moved to *Acton* in 1961. When he was old enough he drank in *The White Hart* pub, filled with the famous and the infamous. Little Terry Nelhams, lived in the flats down the road, used to work at *Rank Screen Services,* told everyone he was going to be a star. Changed his name and the rest, they say, is history. Micky Bruen used to tell people: *Hey, I used to drink with Adam Faith.* Another regular customer was William Hartnell: *Doctor Who,* little fella but what charisma! Famous folk, mixing with the thieves and scallywags and low-life gangsters. Men like Mustapha Cripps who ruled *Acton* like it was his personal property, big-time thief who employed some resourceful and devious accomplices. Henry Akouta was one: Leafy Trees was another. Akouta was the muscle, handy with the knife and the gun. Trees was the brains of the outfit, second-in-command but was always telling Mustapha Cripps how best to run the operation. Leafy Trees was instrumental in the *Group 4* heist in *Hammersmith* in 1975. Akouta had his chance to escape, wanted to show the crowds that he could use a gun, ended up on the main road with a bullet in his throat. Cameras caught Trees and Cripps bang to rights. Two days on the run before Cripps was caught, another day and Leafy Trees was caught. The money, the amount never disclosed, disappeared.

Micky Bruen heard all about the *Group 4* robbery, wanted a piece of the money. Put two and two together and knocked on Leafy's door, pretended he was a friend of Mustapha Cripps, tried to befriend Leafy's wife, Agnes, wormed his way into her skinny heart, reckoned she would know where the stolen loot was hidden. A month of wining and dining and the old girl never said a word, apart from the odd gasp when he took her to her bed. A proper little nun was Agnes Trees, a right Geordie Girl, cute as a cucumber, called one day and she was gone and not a word to Micky Bruen. Neighbour told him she'd gone back to the North-east, didn't get a crust out of Agnes Trees.

Three months later and Micky was in the dock for G.B.H. No big deal for Micky Bruen. Broke some cokehead's nose and teeth but the sentence was savage, even his brief said as much. Five years behind bars, Durham. Then his luck changed, thought he'd been kissed by an angel. On the same block, the one and only Leafy Trees himself. Caught him alone in his cell, bluffed him when he said he knew where his wife was, wanted Leafy to be generous, split the proceeds, Micky was never a greedy man. *Down the middle, Leafy, or I'll split you down the middle!* Days later, Micky Bruen was unconscious, felled from behind when he was taking a leak. Out of action for six long and painful months, fractured skull, steel plate down the left side of his face, teeth missing, squashed vertebrae, leading to nerve-damage all down his right arm. But that was nothing to the mental damage of losing the end of his penis. *All the broken tiles, Mr. Bruen. Someone hitting you, jumping on you, broken tiles as sharp as blades, your member exposed. The full weight of your attacker squashing your penis against the serrated tiles. We tried to repair but there's only so much that cosmetic surgery can do, Mr. Bruen. Mr. Bruen you must stop crying.*

Micky Bruen drove back to the big pub: *The Devon. Dumb name for a pub in Hartlepool,* thought a revived and refreshed Micky, bought the few regulars beers and shorts, five minutes and he knew in which direction to head. Five maybe six miles north, Blackhall Colliery, that would be easy enough to remember, place was full of the black stuff, coal and colliers, then Horden Colliery, colliery after colliery. He remembered the movie, Michael Caine, bollock naked and holding the shotgun playing the tough guy. Good film too, the beach scene, the conclusion, Cockney Cain running about Blackhall beach dodging the aerial-flights as the coal-slag was dumped at sea, then targeted by the hit-man. Micky Bruen grinned. *Could be me,* he thought. *Only I'm better-looking and I won't get shot!*

He parked the *Mini* close to the Trust pub, wandered to the rear-door, glanced across the side-street at the fish-shop. *Warren Fisheries,* said the sign, could he be that lucky? He walked into the pub, his mood cheerful and optimistic, fingers crossed; he might even get bed and breakfast.

CHAPTER SIXTEEN

Almost twenty one days and nights and still the pain of loss tortured and plagued Cornelius Robinson to distraction. The initial days were part-endured with a deep sense of shock. He worked, ate, slept, even had the occasional night of revelry with his friends then, gradually, the reality started to burn him. Slow at first and his initial reaction was that of anger and quick-temperedness then the resentment was eclipsed by irritation and then withdrawal. He made excuses to his acquaintances and stayed at home. Awoke one day, maybe two weeks after she'd told him to leave and knew he could not face work. Fought with the internal demons all the way to the colliery, stood for ages looking at the building, his work-place, an important part of his life, couldn't go on. Still pretended even when work-mates passed him, *Come on, Corky, you've got to clock-on, yer'll miss the cage, man!* Somehow he could smile at them, push then away with a demented leer, *Bad with the beer, youngun', might have a shift off,* then he turned and was walking along the streets in a daydream of sorrow.

The youth could not get Anna out of his mind, loved her so very much and always thought she felt the same, told him so many times, *Couldn't live without you, Corky. Love you, Corky, want to get married, Corky.* He had walked for hours, so long that his mother assumed he'd had an early shift from the pit. He'd been out of the house for three hours then she noticed his unopened lunch-box, still didn't immediately understand. Mavis Robinson handed a cup of tea to her son, tousled his hair affectionately and realized his beautiful locks were dry, hadn't been showered, hadn't been to the colliery. *Corky, are you okay son*? and when he looked at her with that awful pained expression, Mavis gasped, tears filled her eyes, *What's the matter, son, what's happened, Corky*?

"Can't live without her, Ma," the words came out in a whisper, told her he was tired and wanted to sleep, left the room and walked slowly up the narrow stairs but he was neither tired nor sleepy.

After two days alone in his bedroom, not eating nor sleeping, despite verbal and physical efforts from his parents, Mavis Robinson called the surgery. Dr. Johnson, overworked and underpaid, prescribed tranquilizers, *Librium.* Told him to eat well and sleep as much as he wanted and promised to call back within a few days. Corky took the required dosage but still found no peace, his head bursting with an incessant chronic energy. He paced the floor night and day, a manic *Duracell* mannequin at night; a solar-powered dummy during the day.

On the night of the second day he told his parents he felt a little better, wanted to walk away his ghosts. He did, walked like his life depended on it, a marathon man as he strode for all he was worth. Peterlee, Shotton, Haswell Moor then a hard-right at the *Pemberton Arms* and the long unlit road towards Easington Village, skirting the village, hurried down the coastal route, *Seaside Lane,* towards the colliery, resting only when he had reached the outskirts of the place. Found the council seat opposite *The Rock Garden*, new title for the ancient *Trust,* Corky smiled to himself for the first time in days. It was as if an unknown edict existed that demanded every colliery have at least one pub called the *Trust.* The building looked subdued and far removed from its grand and funky new name. On the gable-end was the huge, plastic motif of a guitar with the crescent-shaped announcement: *The Rock Garden. A*part from the scant whispers of grey voltage lifting from the deserted bar-area, the enormous pub was empty. Corky sat for ages and watched the lonely man behind the bar-counter, saw him twice check his watch and once walk hesitantly to the big window, the briefest of looks at the gloom and blackness and then he was back behind the counter, the newspaper grasped and the head lowered. The young voyeur seemed mesmerised by the resoluteness of the middle-aged owner, shook his head at the steely stubbornness of the man who had patience and strength. *No customers tonight, mister,* thought Corky, *why don't you pack in and go home, put out the lights, scream to the bloody heavens that you've not made a penny-piece and go home.* Corky Robinson left the seat and walked towards Horden, his spirits, although rock-bottom, were no longer on self-destruct. He strode past the small hamlet known as *Grants House* and kept thinking about the lone barman doggedly fighting adversity, trying to earn a living and put a crust on the table, strong in his resolve at making a living despite the competition from all the other pubs and clubs around him. Corky wanted to be like the man, wanted to suck some of his strength into his own head, the youth talking out loud: *Once The Trust, now The Rock Garden, next year if the takings don't lift what would be the new name?* Corky Robinson walked towards the *Crossroads* trying to think of a suitable name for the struggling pub.

At the *Crossroads* junction he saw the lights of the lonely grocery/off-license on the opposite side of the road and suddenly felt hungry for something, anything: chocolate or crisps and a drink. Corky Robinson was suddenly ravenous and parched. The traffic was heavy so he stood patiently and waited, saw the big *Volvo* skid on to the parking area in front of the shop and knew before anyone left the vehicle who owned it. Only Dimonti had the kind of brass to afford the foreign car, read the registration number: R D 500. *Arrogant bastard,* thought Corky and he watched the two giggling and excited females leave the motor and walk towards the brightly-lit shop. It was Anna, Anna and her sister, Milly. He stood staring as the car impatiently gunned it's engine, stared dumbly when the two girls hurried from the premises carrying the laden bags, heard the loud *chink chink* as bottles clashed loudly together in the bags, still watching as the *Volvo* zoomed away into the *Crossroads* estate. The hunger had evaporated and he started to walk the short distance home.

The small Peugeot 205 braked hard. The passenger-door was opened, the groan and grind of rust was loud and raw, made Corky smile. His Dad, the budding mechanic, *Chip-fat on the hinges, Corky, just as effective as the real thing.* Now the car not only squealed but smelled.

"Cornelius?" Bart Robinson cocked his head sideways and stared at the lone pedestrian, "Ma was gettin' worried, lad, you want a lift, eh?"

"Knackered, dad," sighed Corky. Exhausted but not on the brink any more, he climbed into the motor, thankful for the rest. Anna was in his thoughts still but the picture was changing. Reality was kicking in making slow headway into his thoughts. He would never stop loving her but he was starting to realise that life with the erratic and explosive Anna would not have worked. Too flighty, too flirty, she would destroy him surely, belittle and degrade and embarrass him until his pride was nothing but a rank memory.

"You okay, son?" Bart was concerned about his son. "Duane's called again, think he's a bit worried about you."

Duane Chambers was Corky's best friend, grew up together, school together, mates for life. He'd asked Duane to be his best man.

"I seem to be upsettin' everybody these days."

"You wanna talk or what?" Barty out of his head with worry about his only son, his pride and joy, a mirror-image of his old man, still couldn't find the right words to say. "Fancy a pint, son, maybe have a bit crack-on about things, eh?"

"No need, dad," said Corky, "honest. I'm okay."

"Sure you are, son," said the father thinking wistfully that his son was actually on the mend. "Tell you what, if you want, I'll call at the fish-shop, cheese-pattie and chips, eh?"

They drove through the colliery in silence, reached the shop, then the surprise for the adult as his son climbed out of the Peugeot, turned and told his dad he was buying for everyone. The hint of a smile as he said casually, *I'll get the usual dad, eh?* The Robinson family special: tail-end for Ma, corned-beef pattie for Bart, cheese-pattie for Corky and three big bags of chips: light on the salt, soaked with vinegar. *Okay, son. I'll wait in the car, I fancy a smoke.* The older man watching as his son walked into the shop, chatting to Brenda and Joan. *Getting better,* he thought, *definitely on the mend.*

Bart looked into the shop, watched Joan Belling. She was a nice kid, nicest kid out of the whole family and so different from Anna. Bart didn't like Anna, she was a whore like her mother, Milly. Before she married, Milly Chandler had a reputation second to none in Horden. She was known as the village-bike. There were few men in the colliery who hadn't ridden Milly. She had to detour to Easington when she wanted to find a fool enough to marry her, not that the marriage contract put any restraint on the girl, messed around with half the men in Horden. Anna was the double of her mother with morals of a bitch, broke Bart's heart when his son announced that he was seeing Anna Belling, had to bite his tongue, couldn't say a word. Kids! You tell them not to see someone and what do they do, bloody forbidden fruits and they end up marrying them. Bart kept quiet hoping it would fizzle out and the opposite happened. Corky decided he wanted to move in with Anna. For a time his son was happy, best he'd been for ages, used to call in after work. A few minutes chat before going to Anna's house and Corky as bright as a button. Bart was starting to think maybe he'd misjudged her, thought perhaps Anna had turned over a new leaf. Pigs fly! She used him and when she was sick of him and wanted another beau, binned him and replaced him in an instant, leaving a distraught Corky to pick up the pieces of his life, going through hell and high water as he tried to forget the little temptress.

Bart had just passed the *Volvo* owned by Ryan Dimonti, saw the two bitches climbing inside the motor as the low-life blasted his car-horn. One was Anna. He had recognised her. Only hoped Corky hadn't seen her, standing nearby and then stumbling along the road like some wandering tramp. His pride and joy fretting over scum like her. Corky could do better, good-looking kid like Cornelius could snap his fingers and find the queue waiting and all better than the Belling girl. Good riddance to bad rubbish he thought, let her find someone of her own ilk, like the scum Dimonti. Anna and Dimonti, yeah, two peas in a pod, both poison, both full of bile and piss. They suited each other down to the ground.

He had known Dimonti his whole life, went to the same school as his dad. There was something odd about John Dimonti, always the loner, on the outside, never the mixer, quiet, calculating and always on his guard. All the kids playing football or cricket and John, lucky if he watched, never participated, wandered the school-grounds on his own. Everyone thought he was weird, left school and stayed only a few years at the pit. Rumours circulated that some of his work-mates found him masturbating in the pit-showers. Nothing wrong with a little pull of the old handle when things are frustrating but there's a time and a place for things like that, it's all about control and John Dimonti was lacking in that department.

Then some years later and married, he fills the Hartlepool Mail with headlines and not the kind of headlines you'd write home about. *Local man caught in police sting in Middlesborough. Money for sex scandal for young father!* They were a few in the colliery sympathetic with the man. *Understandable*, they said, *frustration can bend your sensible head, sleeping with someone who, for whatever reasons, doesn't share the intimacies of a good wholesome marriage can wreck and ruin anyone*. Three years later and similar headlines, Northern Echo and the Hartlepool Mail ran the main story about John Dimonti and the headlines copied blatantly from the film. *The Italian Stallion, The Horden Stallone!* The Peterlee Star went one better, *The Colliery Casanova!* Caught once and you could blame it on bad luck, twice and you're a fool. Dimonti was a fool and a half.

Ryan Dimonti wasn't a chip off the old block, He was the whole damn fence, arrogant and rude; self-opinionated and violent. Few at the colliery liked the lad. He was a thief, caught by Willie Tapping, mechanic, rifling through his haversack, cried and screamed his innocence, threatened Willie with his dad. Willie Tapping laughed at the threats, told the youth he would fight father and son together. Willie Tapping was a tough guy, slapped Ryan Dimonti when he discovered his tools in the lad's haversack who still had the nerve to deny the theft. *I don't fucking know how two screwdrivers and a wrench got in my pockets, I think you planted them, you bald bastard! Wait till my dad gets his hands on you!* Willie belted him, chased him and belted him again, should have been the end of the matter. After all, the matter had been resolved, at least for Willie, should have been for Ryan Dimonti too. One week later, however, next to the pit-baths, Willie Tapping's new *Honda* was petrol-bombed. The culprit was never found but everyone knew who had destroyed the motor. It got worse. Willie bought a Vauxhall, parked it in one of the side-streets near the pit, close but not too close, finished his shift at midnight, started the *Cavalier* and set off for home, everything fine and dandy until he reached the main road near the *Bell*, applied the foot-brake. Nothing! His boot pushed right to the floor as he slipped straight into the *United* bus. The *Vauxhall* was a write-off, the bus was badly scratched and scrapped, Willie, luckily, was unhurt physically but that was enough for Willie Tapping to put his notice in at the colliery and move several miles away. New job, new home, he'd had enough of Ryan Dimonti, anyone crazy enough to cut the brake-pipes on his car was someone to steer clear of.

Then there was the incident with Freddie Cole. Freddy, thirty years old, loved his grub more than he loved life, five feet four and as wide as he was tall. The obese Freddie never made it to the coal-face, never had a look-in, couldn't stoop to save his life. His poor wife Betty, as big as a house herself, had for years fussed over her husband. *The way to a man's heart is through his belly*, she preached and Betty practised what she preached. He was full of fun was Freddie Cole, used to joke when he was sitting perched on the bench at the club that he'd never seen his little willy for years, said Betty couldn't find it either. Freddie Cole was an inoffensive, jolly man who worked on the *transfer-points* underground, cleaning the occasional spillage when the conveyor-belts carrying coal spilt the odd rubbish, did a bit of shovel-work. Transfer-point attendant, a job for the old, knackered and damaged, or for the likes of Freddie Cole.

Ryan Dimonti, in bad books again for poor behaviour underground, was pulled away from his work-mates and taken off material-work. The management, with union approval, had made him work on his own. That way he couldn't hurt or hinder anyone around him. Ryan was given a spray-nozzle, large tins of white emulsion-paint, several brushes and a large plastic container. The flexible hose was connected to the container; the container was filled with the emulsion. By using a simple lever pressure built up in the container and the paint was ejected through the long hose and out of the nozzle. Magic! Whitewashing was done primarily near to the shaft-bottom or landings, made the place look bright and white, a more comfortable environment in which to work. The pressure from the container meant that the emulsion could reach the high walls and ceilings. The big hand brushes were used for ground work only.

As fate would have it, Ryan was moved to the new *transfer-point* manned by Freddie Cole. The older man enjoyed the company and the gossip from young Ryan, even shared biscuits and cakes with him, let him read the *Sun*. Moved a short distance away while the youth, with the big tin of emulsion propped on the steel tables that held the conveyor-belt, busied himself with the job in hand. Then fate intervened. Freddie, studying the racing-form on the back pages of the newspaper did not see the approaching lights of several men. One of the lights was a spot-light - reserved for Deputies and Over-men. Pit officials. Only yards away and Freddie, yawning, glanced up from the *Sun* and saw, too late, the official, up like a dumpy jack-in-the-box Freddie grabbed at his shovel and hurried to the conveyor, rammed his shovel between the river of laden rubber and the steel-table supporting it. Lifted the dust and muck and deposited it on the rumbling belt, kept moving down the line, wanted to show he could work, needed to impress the approaching bosses. Moved again, closer to the youth on the opposite side of the conveyor, pushed the wide shovel across the steel base and heard the *Clank* as metal hit metal. The shovel caught the large tin of paint, the paint overturned and belched gallons of white emulsion over the amazed youth. Nothing for some seconds, Freddie looking frantically at Ryan and Ryan, eyes wide with anger and incredulity, gaped at Freddie. Then it happened, Ryan Dimonti lost all reason as his temper exploded. Over the moving belt like *Superman* he hurtled into the gasping wheezing figure of Freddie Cole, down they went as Ryan battered and kicked at the shrieking older man. Blood and teeth flying as Ryan Dimonti was dragged from the unconscious Freddie. One of the colliers struggling with the youth, was the under-manager of the pit, Sidney Locke. *Get the hell out of this pit, now! Get your bloody cards and go!* Ryan Dimonti`s last day at the mine. Ryan left. Freddie Cole left. Ryan sacked and poor Freddie damaged enough never to work again.

"Dad!" shouted a smiling Corky, his arms laden with the hot food and two large bottles of *Cherryade,* "open the door, Dad."

Bart Robinson grinned broadly. *Better off without her son, he thought, let Dimonti be tortured!* "Give me a minute, give me a minute, will yer!"

"Guess what, Dad, you'll never believe what's happened at the fish-shop?" Corky struggled to climb into the car, his face beaming.

"Givin' away free food?"

"Doug's sold the shop!"

"Pakis?"

"Naw!"

"Indians?"

"Joan has bought it," said Corky, "Anna's sister is the new owner!"

Bart chuckled, "Might get a proper bag of chips now, that bloody Doug was a tight-fisted bugger."

CHAPTER SEVENTEEN

Tyler Chandler was on a roll. Weekends were always sweet but this day was one of the best he'd had. He'd started early, Dimonti had phoned him and demanded his presence. Tyler obeyed and was knocking at the door in McGuiness Avenue within minutes of his summons. Ryan Dimonti was not a man to upset. He still remembered the brief altercation with the gangster a year ago. Tyler must have caught him on a bad day because all he did was answer back, next minute and he was on the floor with the spiky-haired freak straddling him, screaming so loud that spittle covered Tyler's flinching face. That wasn't the worst part, Dimonti had stuck a pistol in his ear, pushed so hard it made his eyes water. Story of his life really, one cock-up after another..........

Tyler had been man-handled most of his life. People knew he could not use his fists. He was a coward and would rather run than fight. When he was a child his Dad would beat him, any excuse and he was thrashed, only him. His sister Milly was never touched. Grew up hating his father and his sister, took a long time but he repaid both of them. Stole from his Dad, played around with his sister's kids. Repaid them both in full.

Tyler hated pain, especially when it was inflicted on him. He had tried to be a tough guy when he was younger. Not long out of school, working at the colliery, bullying anyone who was suckered by his manic behaviour. The ploy worked for a while, especially when he was frightening younger kids. Tyler screamed a lot in those days, upped the tempo half-way through any argument then suddenly started ranting and raving like a lunatic, grabbed people and shook them to death. Worked a treat for a few years, everyone thought he had a tile loose. Tyler would walk around the colliery like he owned it.

He was King of the Colliery but only in his own warped mind. Tyler started believing his own reputation, all swagger and show as he started to build on his dubious reputation and attended Karate classes at the Community-Centre in Peterlee. Preferred it to boxing. Boxing was far too physical for Tyler Chandler. He found the martial-arts a doddle, easy-peasy, learning a few deft moves, play-acting like he knew what he was doing. Let everyone know he was a skilled and dangerous craftsman: Ah, Grasshopper, he would ease into the conversation, pretending to be David Carradine, tell people he was a black-belt; occasionally a black-belt, Second-Dan.

Then it all changed, spin of a coin and his reputation was in tatters. Twenty-two at the time, out of work so he was buying and selling. Dimonti was a nobody then so Tyler had to travel to Easington to buy poppers and assorted shit from Ernie Johnstone. Sometimes he would call in the off-licence and buy a crate of cider in case Ernie was short of the basics. The school-kids loved the booze and paid him a fortune. Eight-o-clock and Tyler was lugging two carrier-bags of booze towards the recreation-ground, a popular meeting-place for the teenies.

Some little kid objected to the high prices and started bad-mouthing Tyler. The drug-dealer, ten years older and twice the size of the school-kid, *slaps the punk across the face, knocked him on his back. Let that be a lesson to you, kid. You know who you are dealin' with, eh, Tyler Chandler!* Those were the last words he said. The youngster, small and slight, was up like a wild animal, his fists like pistons as they put holes in Tyler's ego. Over in seconds, the older man screaming for mercy, the kid pummelling him like he was a punch-bag, the youngster having the final laugh. *You know who I am, Mister? Marlon McGintey and I can fight anyone!*

Tyler's Cowardly Lion act was soon over, he quickly stopped bawling and threatening folk, especially when he was liable to be assaulted. Changed his routine and backed off from any kind of confrontation, unless he was certain of success, usually women or kids, depending on their size and age and adopted an easy-going dumb approach. Tyler covered himself in a coating of Teflon, ducked and dived and rarely got stuck in any awkward situation. He survived okay, made a living..............

The afternoon trade in Peterlee had been unexpectedly busy. Tyler had called on all the local known pubs that catered to the wild crowd and had been disappointed. *The Butterfly* was deserted and he almost took a slow ride back to Horden, then decided at the last moment to call in at the *The Royal Arms*. The pub was choc-a-bloc with kids with money to burn. Within half an hour Tyler Chandler emerged from the toilets, convinced he was infested with lavatory stench but happy that he'd off-loaded half of his load. Then he'd called at the town-centre, first the *Norseman Hotel* which was empty, crossed the road and entered the *Gamecock* and hit the bulls-eye, sold the rest of the shit in minutes, downed a double whiskey to celebrate then tried his luck with the local fillies. An hour later and a wedge of his profit wasted attempting to woo the talent and he gave it up as a bad job. *What was it with bitches?* He asked himself as he booked a taxi to Horden Crossroads and Dimonti. He had the looks, the personality and the money, could not understand his lack of success with the opposite sex. Tyler ordered a big refill, needed it for the long night ahead. *Who cared,* he thought, *there was always the kiddies.*

****

Jackie Brown had severed all links with Ryan Dimonti. He'd found the courage to drive the short distance to McGuiness Avenue and confront the gangster. *What the fuck you mean, you want out? This is the thanks I get for loading you with money, eh? You bite the hand that feeds you, you moron!* Jackie took all the shit and bile from the little man with a smile. He was no longer afraid of him. He'd seen Dimonti in a real crisis and saw the mettle of the man. It was all a front. Jackie Brown was moving on. The dark side of life was being abandoned. The everyday deals with low-life scum were going to be a thing of the past. The inner rage that he had carried almost all of his life was starting to recede. No longer did he wish to carry the mantle of tough-guy or Mister Fix-It, it wasn't worth the grief. *Met somebody, Mr. Dimonti, want to settle down. Want a life. Never had a life, never had a proper home. You understand that, Mr. Dimonti, never had a proper home until now?* He stood as the criminal slammed the door in his face, stood and listened as the man shouted obscenities and threats. *You'll be back, moron! Couple a weeks and you'll be knocking on my door, moron! Get the fuck outa here, you big dumb oaf!*

He owed it all to Joan. Joan had saved him from a life of crime. The robbery at Elemore Hall, he had convinced himself, was the sweet kiss of fate. The death of poor Agnes Trees was blamed on Dimonti and Anna. They were incompetent and stupid. Had Jackie Brown been allowed to organize the robbery he would have worked around Agnes, would have somehow plotted and bypassed her, would have made certain that she was out of the house if he'd been given the task to plan the burglary. The death of Leafy Trees's wife was not his fault and he had no conscience about it. The money, the thousands made, was his by right, he deserved the loot. Jackie Brown had saved Leafy's skin and without his intervention Micky Bruen would have destroyed the old burglar in the prison. He was owed, big time and all he had done was call in his debts. So now he had money enough to start his new life with the best girl in the whole wide world.

****

Ten-o-clock and the Bell was heaving, the lounge was bursting to capacity. The punters, all young and excited filled the place, packed like sardines in a tin, drinks nestling on chests, shoulder to shoulder. Sweet bedlam as the music blared so loud it drowned any hope of normal conversation. Shouting and miming and head-nodding was the Friday-night norm, all too much for Corky Robinson and Duane Chambers as they pushed and prised their way to the corridor and the bar, the place still busy but almost normal with the counter littered with seasoned punters who enjoyed the drink and the conversation.

Months ago and Corky had asked Duane to be his best man. Only months and Corky had been ecstatic. *I'm getting married Duane,* he'd confided in his friend. *Anna wants to marry me!* It still rankled Duane the way his friend had been used and abused by the Belling girl, almost cost him his friendship when he discovered Corky's feelings for Anna Belling, should have held his tongue and kept his thoughts to himself, cared about him too much to keep quiet. He had been proved right and it hurt him to see the depressed state of his pal. *Corky.* He had begged for days when he'd heard about the split, *you've got to get out of the damn house. Please, man, have a drink with me.* Corky and Duane, socializing for the first time in an age, Duane pleased as punch, Corky determined to overcome the heartache. *One day at a time,* said Duane, *that's all it takes to mend.*

The snooker table was empty and the pair, with a little persuasion from Duane, decided to play.

131

"You okay?" Duane was still concerned about his friend.

"Pleased to be out," Corky shrugged his shoulders, "take my mind off all the bother."

"Back at work yet?"

"Monday, Duane," he replied, stooped, toyed with the cue, said, "£1 a game?" then fired the ball into the pocket.

"You're on."

"Anna's got my gear still," off the cuff and casual from Corky as he stepped back and allowed his friend to play.

"Much?"

"Stereo and television," Corky Robinson was fishing for advice from his only friend.

"Let it go, Corky, not worth the hassle."

"You reckon?"

Two females, still with drinks in their hands, sauntered in from the lounge, saw the youths and smiled. Twins: Fiona and Felicity Fuller, identical apart from the hair, Fiona was blonde, Felicity was copper and both beautiful.

"There's Corky Robinson," said Felicity, "recognise that arse anywhere."

"Forget it," replied her sister, "he's shacked up with Anna Belling."

"So?"

"Anna will choke you if she finds out."

"Shut up and follow me!"

Duane nudged his pal, still spread-eagled over the snooker table; Corky turned, smiled and played the shot blind, the balls bounced everywhere. He straightened up and acknowledged the girls.

"Distracted him, girls," sighed Duane, shook his head and feigned annoyance, "and him single again, footloose and fancy-free."

"Hello, Corky," said Felicity, attempting to stick her small chest out without making it too obvious.

"Long time, Felicity."

"Is it true?"

"About what?" asked the lad. He eyed the female and tried to push aside the images of Anna. It was so difficult.

"Anna and you?"

"All over," replied Corky glumly, "it's just one of those things."

"Celebrating or commiserating?" replied Felicity, draining her glass, looking at the dour face of Cornelious Robinson. She winked and smiled. *What a waste,* she thought, *fretting over Anna Belling.* "It's not the end of the world, Corky, you don't get fined for smiling."

Corky Robinson smiled, shrugged his shoulders. *What the hell,* he thought.

"It's a celebration," interrupted Duane, glancing at his friend, observed the smile "and the drinks are on me!"

"Then I'll have a rum and coke," said the girl.

"Mine's a lager and lime," said Fiona, turning to Duane Chambers, "make that a pint and I'll give you a kiss."

There was commotion in the nearby corridor, the door flew open and an irate bouncer was man-handling Tyler Chandler. They struggled into the bar, the door-man accusing, the smaller man denying. The racket was loud and aggressive. Tyler recognized the youth standing next to the billiard table.

"Corky," begged Tyler Chandler, arms outstretched as he tried in vain to reach the youth, "Tell him, Corky, he thinks I'm sellin' shit!"

Maurice Whitehouse looked at the group, acknowledged the two youths, said, "Corky, this prick was in the cubicle with a punter, second time tonight. He's either pushin' or playin'."

"He's a skip-rat," growled Corky Robinson.

"Give me a break, Corky!" pleaded Tyler. He'd made a fortune for Dimonti, the drunks had queued all night outside the lavatory and he had about £20 worth of shit left, the last thing he wanted was to trail round Horden finding another pub. Half an hour tops and he'd sell the rest of the stuff.

"You're scum, Chandler," grunted Corky Robinson, "like Anna. You both piss in the same pot!"

Still protesting vehemently, Tyler Chandler was dragged out of the pub. Duane looked at his friend, stuck his thumb up and smiled. Corky was on the road to recovery.

CHAPTER EIGHTEEN

Friday was extremely busy for the young couple. The shop was heaving with customers, the delivery car, a three-year old *Datsun Cherry* bought the previous day for cash, had never stopped delivering. Tuesday they had run out of fish so Joan persuaded Jackie Brown to drive to Newcastle quay-side to purchase several boxes of cod, five in the morning and Jackie was bursting with vigour and happiness. He returned by eight, went straight to the preparation-room and by nine-o-clock the work for the day had been completed. He scrubbed the filth and grime off his hands and ran up the private staircase to the flat. He could smell the bacon, saw Joan singing softly next to the cooker and moved to her side, his powerful arms wrapping around her slim and perfect frame.

"Happy?" he gushed, didn't care any more if he looked and sounded like a love-sick fool. His life had irrevocably changed for the better and he felt reborn, not only in love with the most caring and beautiful woman in the world but in love with life. He'd never known such elation or bliss, wanted to tell the world about his sublime change of fortune; scream it from the rooftops. *Look at me, I've found love. I've discovered peace and contentment, the all-new Jackie Brown. Born again Jackie Brown!*

Joan turned and faced him, snuggled into the enormous girth and felt warm and protected, didn't have to say a single word to her big giant of a man.

****

"They're calling in to see you, Ryan?" said Anna, cute as a kitten and as cunning as a snake. She had insisted Ryan take back all of the money she had earned for the robbery at

Elemore Hall. Played an ace and won, day after and he was helping her unload her bags. *Men,* she thought, *so gullible.*

"Yeh, they've been away," he answered, "holiday, kinda."

"Anywhere nice?" Anna asked like she cared. *As if!*

He had told her about his parents, Nichola and John Dimonti, born and bred in the North-East of England. Three generations centred in or around the small colliery and before that, Barnard Castle. Durham folk lumbered with the strange Italian surname. Nichola was not in the best of health and for as long as Ryan could remember she had been wheel-chair bound. In hospital, out of hospital; operation after operation, curvature of the spine, the specialists said. Deteriorated over the last few years as the walking turned into plodding then to an unsightly gait as Nichola gamely limped and shuffled then the discomfort and pain made artificial mobility a necessity. Young Ryan used to enjoy the fun and games when both he and his mother held on for dear life as John Dimonti hurled through the back streets playing racing-cars and dodgems, happy days for the young boy, oblivious to the embarrassment and pain of chronic ill-health.

"Scarborough."

Excitement City, thought the girl, full of her own selfish ignorance. "Strange choice," she answered and continued with the preparation of the lunch. Brunch actually, it was gone noon and they'd been out of bed for only minutes.

"Same boarding-house, Anna," he said, "all mod-cons to help Ma, you know, ramps and things?"

Not interested in anyone but herself, the girl asked, "You want fried bread as well as bacon, eggs and beans?" The man ate till he burst and didn't put on an ounce. *Had to be the metabolism,* thought Anna.

"Is that a problem, Anna?" Ryan Dimonti was trying to read the Northern Echo.

What was the world coming to, he thought, first Jackie Brown reneging on his promises. *Do anything for you Mr. Dimonti. Need the work, Mr. Dimonti,* then he shows his worth with the raid on Leafy's place. Dimonti had to admit that the big oaf had some cool moves, then, out of the blue, the dope falls in love, so what was the big deal? *Fall in love with anyone you want, Primo, even Anna's goofy sister but don't give up the day-job, eh?* Wants to try his luck selling fish and chips. *Are you kidding me, Jackie Brown, eh? Now I'll have to think of something to get him back on board.*

Then Percy Willetts, number-two heavy, who used to be number-one until Primo showed his potential, was banged up in Peterlee nick for slapping his missus about. Percy, even though he didn't know it, was going down for some months. Thought he was down to nil with heavies, thought maybe he'd have to act as his own muscle for some time and then he has a change of luck. Alex Bunty, barman at the *Trust* phones and says some big guy is looking for work. *Shall I send him over, Ryan, he looks kinda useful?* Dimonti thinks, why not have a look and a talk to the stranger? *Micky Bruen is the name, Mr. Dimonti, up from the Smoke for a while until things calm down. Anything you want me to do, you phone the Trust, eh?* Told him he'd think about it, not wanting to appear too keen. That was two days ago, contacted him yesterday: *Come tomorrow night, Micky Bruen. Saturday suits me, about six.* Every cloud has a silver lining, eh? Swings and roundabouts and all that shit? Lose Jackie and Percy, no sweat, tonight we'll see what the Londoner can do.

"You wanna eat in the kitchen," asked Anna, "or in front of the television? *What was it with men and football,* thought the girl, *boys until they die!* "Ryan, you hear me?"

He hurried into the kitchen. "They've arrived, Anna," said Ryan, "we'll eat later, eh. You go and put some clothes on, look more the part, Ma is a bit old-fashioned."

Shaking her head, she dutifully left the room and climbed the stairs. *What was it with men and football and mothers*? The nightgown was definably risqué but she was wearing the dressing-gown. What was the problem? Fuming silently to herself, Anna quickly started dressing, glanced out of the bedroom-window and saw the fellow open the boot and lift out the invalid-carriage, a quick flick of his arms and the contraption cranked open. Now he was moving towards the passenger-side, opening the door and helping the woman as she struggled on to the wheel-chair. He was slim and fit, average height, salt and pepper hair, thick still and swept back over his face and sported a thin, well-manicured beard. His wife looked older, heavy-set and Anna could see she was losing her hair, from the window the scalp shone pink through the receding foliage. Anna found old-age distressing. *Jesus, don't let me end that way.* She took perhaps a minute before she'd finished dressing, recalled Ryan's words about his mother, *Old-fashioned,* thought Anna, *probably believes in marriage too.* Wondered how she could possibly fit the topic into the conversation, smiled to herself as she hurried down the stairs. She would find a way.

Anna in the living-room, waiting, Ryan in the kitchen, watching: his father struggling with the wheel-chair, hoisting the carriage up the few back-steps, the man's back patchy with perspiration from the exertions. He reversed out of sight for just a moment as he manipulated the carriage, heard Ryan attempt humour, *Passed your driving-test, dad, got to signal before you move, eh?*

The Dimonti trio entered the room, father joking with the son and the woman staring pensively at Anna. Anna trying her best to look happy, big smile for mammy and daddy Dimonti.

"Anna," said a breezy Ryan, grinning at the sight of Anna, "meet the parents."

There was something wrong, Anna's head was heading skyways in abject amazement, her past rearing its ugly head, stood and gaped. Her young body shook with a shock-wave of fright. It wasn't the woman, she wasn't looking at the seated figure, Anna's gaze settled on the man, Ryan's father. It was the eyes she remembered, the trim beard and when he spoke, her heart chilled and shuddered involuntary, her mask was down, her guard gone. She could not hide her distress.

"Nice to meet you Anna," said a friendly soft-spoken John Dimonti, eased his frame from around the carriage and held out his hand but already he was frowning. He witnessed the garish blush of crimson spreading across the face of the girl and tried to stay calm. His hand began to shake.

Anna Belling was in another place.

Years ago and Uncle Tyler smiling his ferret smile. *Anna, this is Mr. Brown. I've told him all about you Anna,* the ten-year old pouting. *He's old, Uncle Tyler. I want to go home.* But she didn't go home. She stayed with Mr. Brown, who was sometimes called Mr. Smith and after a while started to enjoy all the attention from the man. *This is for you, honey, he would say, don't tell Tyler. Now, shall we have our little bath-time, Anna and then I'll dry you in front of the fire and sprinkle talcum-powder all over your cute little body? You'd like that Anna, wouldn't you?*

"Anna?" said a puzzled and rather concerned Ryan Dimonti.

"Pet?" said the old woman leaning out of the carriage and trying to grasp at her slack, limp arms, "is there something wrong?"

The young girl came out her stupor, a child again. She could not stop the laughter, hysterical and high-pitched. Giggled insanely then tears fell as she spoke. *It's Anna, don't you remember me, Mr. Brown? Your little baby?* Then the laughter grew in crescendo, laughter and tears, shrieking and calling out as loud as she could. *Hey, Mr. Brown, want me to sit on your knee, Mr. Brown, want to kiss me with that tickly beard, Mr. Brown!*

Ryan Dimonti and his mother did not comprehend at first. It was only when they turned and looked at John Dimonti, saw the rivers of tears running down his ashen face. It was then that the horror hit them.

CHAPTER NINETEEN

Friday evening. 10.15pm and the twins were ready. Tommy and Tyrone Morrison had spent the whole week planning their revenge. Tommy, wheel-chair bound, had concealed the weapon under the blankets, between his legs. Who would notice the extra bulge and if they did, would they even mention anything to a cripple in a wheelchair? *Hey, Tommy, you not too hot with all those blankets, you want me to tidy-up around you? Chance is, Tommy, you mighta pissed your pants again, eh?* Not in a thousand years would anyone but his constant companion and twin-brother Tyrone, mess with his gears........

They lived together, Tyrone and Tommy Morrison, moved to Easington Colliery after the mayhem and nightmare of the trial, disillusioned and burning with a fevered hatred of the man who had single-handedly destroyed their young lives forever. They lived together behind *Seaside Lane* in an especially-designed bungalow for maimed and crippled colliers. The council and the N.C.B. had come together in a joint act of goodwill and allowed the youths to live there.

Tyrone, the most mobile of the Morrison twins, despite being blind in one eye and with limited vision in the other, had managed to procure the second-hand but very efficient 2.2 rifle. Bobby Murray, a business-friend of the twins had sold them it cheap. Bobby said it was cheap, the going-rate was double what he was charging. Bobby, a petty-thief and drug-addict and the biggest dealer in the colliery, had discovered the weapons weeks earlier. Burgling the farm-house in South Hetton had been easy, watched the whole family leave in the big horse truck; livestock in the rear, living-quarters up front and sharing the cab-space. *Poor farmers*, thought Tommy, as he knelt next to the unruly hedge. He had intended robbing the sheds and byres of anything worth stealing, then he watched gleefully as two adults and the two youngsters - decked out in riding-breeches and hard-hats - clambered into the huge wagon and drove away. Bobby, filled with a false bravado, thanks to the daily intake of *ganja* and the additional free syrup of *methadone,* had rapped loudly at the door. No one came, no dogs barked, the silence was golden, took his time robbing the farm, found a little money under the bed: *Carry all the notes in their bloody deep pockets, poor farmers!* Cheered up when he found the cache of weapons, two shotguns, a 2.2 rifle and a handgun. *Farmers with handguns?* and the ammunition, bags of it. Bobby Murray knew some low-life characters that would pay major money for the guns so his mood lifted. Then he cleared the kitchen of food, bagged it and left, hid the weapons two fields away, took the food home and with the pittance stolen he purchased some quality *blow* that would quadruple in price when he sold it.

Big mistake calling to see the twins but that was Bobby all over, kept his customers and friends well supplied. The boys were well-placed to buy anything off Bobby Murray; the weekly benefits for the Morrison twins were unbelievable, allowances for this, allowances for that: money for this, that and the other. *Shoulda been a cripple myself boys, eh, worth a fortune you two.* Saw the real anger flare across both faces and knew he'd overstepped the mark. *Only a silly joke, boys, nothing nasty intended, eh?* Hit them where it hurt, saw another side to the twins when they chased him out of the bungalow. Did no business for weeks, knocked on their door and was rebuffed. *Fuck off, Bobby,* they cried, *take your shit elsewhere!* Well, bottom line, he was a businessman, needed to get the boys back on board, their money used to be guaranteed every single week. *Listen, Tommy. Tyrone, what say I give you big discounts for a coupla weeks, will that sweeten you?* So they started negotiating when Tyrone comes out with a gem. *Want a rifle, Bobby. You get me a rifle and I'm not talkin' slug-guns here, I'll pay you top price.* And Tommy jumps on the bandwagon too. *You come up with the goods, Bobby and we'll start buyin' again. We got a deal, or what?* Bobby Murray, who could sell sand to the Arabs, could not stand in their way. Bust a gut, but he would find them a rifle. *Hey, boys, you talkin' to the main man! Gimme a few days, gonna cost you a packet but for my favourite customers, you gotta deal!*

Tyrone was running with perspiration. He had pushed the wheel-chair all the way from Easington, reached the *Bell* in Horden and called in for refreshments.

"Gotta stop, Tommy, need to get my breath."

So they paused next to the *Jack Dormand* complex, Tyrone squatting, his head bowed, sucking in the night air. Tommy was staring at the old-people's home, thinking black thoughts.

"We gonna end up there, Tyrone, you think?"

The brother didn't answer immediately. In a few short minutes they would have reached the bend in the road, turn the corner and have sight of their destination, the fast-food place, *Warren Fisheries,* owned by their tormentor, Hovis Brown.

Tyrone Morrison glanced at his brother. "You sure you want to do this?"

"Only thing kept me alive."

"Me too, let's get Hovis Brown!"

****

Micky Bruen knew exactly what to do. He'd spent enough time sizing up the place, peek-a-boo when no one was looking or awake, the premises had a walled enclosure at the rear, the wooden door permanently bolted and locked from the inside. Once a week, the trash was put out, two large plastic waste-bins, early Thursday morning and dragged back inside on the same afternoon then bolted shut.

Micky Bruen had hoisted his big frame onto the wall several times in the evenings, always when the delivery-car had motored away from the place. A beaten-up Datsun, the only new thing on the heap was the lettering. *Warren Fisheries: Delivery-Service.* Right little businessman was Hovis Brown. Something had happened to the dimwit, someone had waved a magic-wand over the gorilla, too many people had said as much about him. *Thick as two short planks,* they had said. *Inbred, that's Hovis. Loony-tune!* That was the usual response about Jackie Brown.

From his vantage point on the wall he could see into the small concrete yard, outside lavatory, probably for the staff, a large kitchen-window and two separate doors, one presumably for the shop, the other had to be the private entry for the upstairs flat. Jackie Brown's love nest. He'd seen the female, above average height, slim and quite a catch. How did the man do it? He was one ugly son-of-bitch. Hovis Brown must have something that pulled in the chicks, wouldn't have it for much longer though.

He'd been in the yard twice. He imagined the couple finishing their shift, locking the rear fish-shop door and then unlocking the entrance to the flat. His initial plan was to hide in the lavatory, wait until they had entered the flat and then make his presence felt. Micky could not believe his good fortune when he discovered that the door to the upstairs-flat was never locked. Twice in the back-yard and each time the door was unlocked. Micky Bruen, naturally, improvised and sneaked into the stairwell, closed the door behind him and made his way slowly to the large rooms above the shop. There he waited patiently on the sofa with the blade in his hand. He had waited a long time for this moment and was going to treasure it. The heavy buzz of the extraction-fan faltered then died, silence for a second then the clashing of doors. The intruder eased to the large double-windows, closed the flimsy curtains then moved behind the door with the knife ready. The door to the flat was opened, the lights shone and the couple were moving and talking. Joan walked into the living-room seconds before Jackie Brown, who was struggling at the bottom of the stairs to engage the door-key.

It happened so fast for the woman. Suddenly a huge shape materialized out of nowhere, someone as big and as powerful as an ox, grabbed her from behind and thrust a cold sharp blade on to her unexposed neck. *Not a word, bitch or I'll slice your neck like a Christmas turkey!* Joan was manhandled across the room until she stood in front of the big sofa. Jackie Brown strode into the living-room then stopped dead in his tracks, stared in amazement at the burglar standing in front of the window, one hand gripped tight on Joan's hair so that her head was arched back, the other hand held the long switch-blade against her neck. Already the tautness from the vice-like grip and the spasms as the woman struggled had made weals and blotches across the white skin.

"Mister," said Jackie Brown, remarkably calm and collected, lifted the cloth money-bag, "It's all here, the takings." He gestured towards the settee, "I'm putting it on the sofa, it's all yours." Like a viper eyeing his next meal, the big man eased gently towards the couch, his stare riveted on the intruder, placed the cloth bag on the nearest cushion and spoke softly to the thief. "Where the television is, I'll pull it away, under the carpet there's a floor safe, the week's takings are there. It's all yours, mister." He lifted his hand and showed the bunch of keys. "Keys to the safe," and placed them next to the cloth sack.

Micky Bruen spoke, said coldly, "You don't know me?"

"No," shook his head and stared forlornly at Joan; shrugged his massive shoulders, "never seen you before in my life, mister."

"Never used to shave my head, Hovis Brown."

Wide dumb stare from Jackie as the realisation hit him. *Can't be him. Jesus Christ!*

"Thought I'd let you see the scars," spat the knifeman, "can't show them all of course, can't show the steel plate in my head, can't show you the remains....."

"Micky Bruen!" gasped an incredulous Jackie Brown.

"Caused some misery, Jackie Brown, reckon you owe me."

"I'm sorry man!"

"Too late for sorry."

"I was doin' someone a favour, they told you wanted a piece of Leafy Trees's arse. Swear to God..."

"You dumb motherfucker, I ain't bent, told Leafy I wanted the money from the *Group 4* job. That was Leafy up to his old tricks again. Uses people, Jackie Brown, Hovis Brown, whatever your dumbfuck name is, gets people to do his dirty work, especially apes like you!"

Joan's eyes were starting to roll with the pressure from the blade, her features were grey, heavy lines of perspiration ran rivulets down her shocked face.

"Let her go, man," pleaded Jackie, "she's done nothing', it's me you want. Cut me, man!"

Micky Bruen started talking, slowly and deliberately. Told in detail about the horrific groin injuries he'd suffered, all the pain and gore, too much for Joan who gave the smallest of gasps then fainted. The intruder eased himself to the floor with her, eyes never for a moment leaving Jackie Brown. Bruen told his captive to sit on the sofa, told him he would cut the girl's throat if he moved a muscle. Jackie obeyed, eyes locked on his adversary trying desperately to think of something. Joan coughed, her mouth opened and closed, her eyes fluttered as if she was having a bad dream, soft moans escaped from her lips. Micky Bruen fumbled in his pocket and pulled out the hand-gun, cocked the trigger and slowly pointed it towards the seated, silent figure then he stood, his glare focusing on the victim, eyes mocking, smile stiff, his arm extended now and aimed at the head of Jackie Brown.

"Waited a long time for this, pal."

"Ain't your pal," said a resolute Jackie Brown. Proud, his mind plagued with a myriad of thoughts and images, *Almost made it, Jackie, almost had a life, Jackie Brown.* He closed his eyes and thought of Joan, the only one he would miss in the whole world, first time he had found true happiness, first time he had found true love.

Bang! The massive explosion echoed through the room.

The single retort seemed to detonate glass then mayhem. Jackie jumped and waited for the pain of death, heard the almost inaudible gasp from the assassin's lips, the crunch and bump as the huge body stumbled into the broken window-glass that had somehow littered the whole carpeted area. Jackie Brown opened his eyes and saw the horror on the face of Micky Bruen, the disbelief and shock as the reality registered, his features clamped on the mushrooming blood that burst from his chest, the fright and astonishment registering as he saw his life ebbing away.

Jackie Brown finally reacted, grabbing at the pistol. He stumbled after the convulsing figure and pushed the gun at the neck of the dying man then he realized the gravity of the would-be assassin's wounds, flung the weapon away and hurried to the prostrate and wheezing figure of Joan. Lifted her like a doll and stormed from the room, down the stairs like a madman ran Jackie Brown, almost bent the door-keys as he frantically opened the door, only stopped when he reached the safety of the yard, blowing and retching like an old bull as he cradled and caressed Joan. *We've made it, love. We've made it*, he cried.

Outside, half a street away, the inept and amateurish killers hurried from the scene. Tommy and Tyrone

Morrison, colliery hit-men! Feverish with the delight of the kill they chattered incessantly.

"Can't believe it Tyrone," gasped an astounded Tommy, "we've done it!"

Tommy, crippled in body but not sight, had been elected to be the shooter. Turning the corner and struggling along the darkened back street they moaned in unison, the shop was in darkness. They both imagined that their only chance at revenge had been lost to them when they discovered the steel shutters already drawn. In abject misery the twins turned to leave but just as quickly as the shop lights were extinguished, the flat above had blossomed into life. The pair quickly recovered their composure as they viewed the outline of the man parading in front of the large window. Ecstatic and elated, they knew they had another chance.

Quickly, Tommy fumbled for the loaded rifle, pulling and tugging to dislodge the gun from the blankets that concealed the weapon, heart banging like a big drum, fingers trembling as he valiantly tried to lift and aim the weapon. Filled with trepidation and fear, his hands shook as he strained with the weight of the gun, then the flood of wet heat burst over his midriff. The catheter had dislodged! *You'll have to do it, Tyrone*, he moaned, *I'm covered in piss! Take it Tyrone!* The gaping figure grasped at the rifle, cocked the weapon and aimed but the figure at the window seemed to drift downwards out of sight. Tyrone lowered the gun in dismay. Both brothers glanced glumly at one another, didn't have to speak, shared the torture of missed opportunity. Suddenly the huge figure of the man seemed to grow into sight again, in full view, larger than life and as plain as day. *Do it, Tyrone, squeeze the bloody trigger!* Tyrone Morrison looked carefully along the barrel using his right eye, could barely distinguish the black shape between the grey blur of the window-pane, finger pulling gently on the trigger, *Bang* and the window and the shadow exploded. The stricken man seemed to fumble and grab at the curtains as he spun with the ferocity of the impact then he collapsed out of sight. *You've bloody done it, Tyrone! You've bloody done it! Bullseye!*

"Pretty-Boy Floyd!" laughed Tyrone.

"Legs Diamond!" shrieked an elated Tommy.

One had the looks, one had the legs and together they made quite a team. At least this night they would sleep the sleep of the contented.

They laughed and cried all the way home.